ISBN (print): 979-8-9873730-7-1

Publisher: Rocket Books LLC

Aim for Love

ALICIA WILDER

MOLLIE

THE TRAIL DIPS DOWN A RAVINE, the single track surrounded by tall grass, then immediately straight back up a rocky hill. It looks challenging. It looks—*maybe?*—impossible.

I don't hesitate. My momentum and peer pressure push me over the ridge, flying through the downhill stretch, then I stand up from my seat to tackle the incline. My thighs burn from the climb. My breath comes in gasps. My heart is going to beat right out of my chest. But I've got it—a bit farther, a little more intensity. *Push!*

Look at the trees lining the trail. So many different colors of wildflowers. It's gorgeous. This distraction works for about 10 seconds. The scenery isn't moving fast enough.

The loud music in my ears urges me on. I try to use my butt muscles, like my instructor said. I'm moving...very...slowly. This is harder than I expected. The pedals are barely moving, and sweat is dripping down my forehead into my eyes. It's still so far. One of my legs is cramping.

I keep going. A little bit at a time, I keep moving up the hill.

Gravity seems to push me back as fast as I can push the pedals. I'm gasping for air.

One word starts to echo through my head: *No.*

This is *too* hard. I'm never going to make it.

No, says my head. And my pounding heart and my cramping legs. *No.*

I hit the button to release the pressure and fly up the remainder of the leg without any resistance, ducking my head as everyone around me in the spin class celebrates reaching the top of the trail shown on the big screen at the front of the room. I don't deserve any celebration. I wimped out. *Again.*

Sophie, on the bike directly in front of me, turns around to whip her towel at me. "That was great! We're going to be so ready for this trip."

Nora, two bikes over, raises her towel in the air and pumps it.

I put my towel over my face and silently scream.

one

HUNTER

I'M READING this book about living slowly that might do some good if I had a copy for everyone this morning. The tourists are always in such a hurry. They vacation in a small, mountain town to get away from their busy, stressful lives but bring all that pressure and impatience with them.

One family is disinfecting every exposed part of their bodies in the corner. Nearby, there's a group of women pouring over the tour schedule with highlighters. And then, as inevitable as time, a dad is coaching his kids—poorly—in front of a guide who knows more about the subject than he does.

We see the same types over and over in the tour business, and some of the guys get pretty cynical about it. That book reminded me to focus on the connections between us.

Whether people are drawn here for peace or adventure, Telluride, a town that changes slowly, tucked between massive mountains that are relatively young, has seen it all. I try to channel that ability to weather anything when tourists get on my nerves—which has already happened on day one.

I chose axe throwing as the first event of the tour. It's a good opportunity to gauge who we're working with, a surprisingly telling activity to see how athletic people are, or at least whether they're body aware and understand kinetic linking.

Warming up my throwing arm, I start drawing the group's focus by practicing a few times, using my own axe. The ones offered here all have nicks in their edge and the weight in the handle feels off to me now that I'm used to my own. It's easy to hit the bullseye every time if you can repeat the same steps with every throw, which my own axe allows me.

And because they know me here, they let me throw some trick shots, such as two axes at the same time.

A group of slack-jawed women have gathered to watch me.

"It's about body memory," I assure them. "Not skill."

That's not 100% true, of course. But it's true enough to give them some hope they can do it. It will help if they understand the concept that energy travels through connected joints and muscles, like a coordinated sequence or links in a chain, to create optimal movement. However, it's impossible to tell by looking at people who's got a background in sports or natural athletic ability. Thus the activity we're about to engage in.

Now that we have the attention of the group, I give the floor to Scott, one of the other guides from Aspen Adventure Center, who goes over basic safety instructions and then asks for a volunteer to go first.

The group of three women start shoving each other, all of them teasingly trying to persuade another to raise their hand.

"Mollie will do it!" blurts the blonde, and the other two push the third in front of them.

The weakest link, I presume. The woman who always ends up with the short stick, or slightly on the outside of group decision making. She's wearing leggings that emphasize her curves, and has a brown pixie cut. She looks more nervous than the casual situation calls for. I smile at her, but she looks sweaty and distracted. Scott and I exchange a brief look.

"Let's not force anyone who's not ready." I wave her off.

"No," she says, surprising me. "I'm ready." She's shaking a little, but she steps forward.

Scott invites her to stand in position in front of the stall, behind the line that's marked 12 feet away from the bullseye. He directs her to put one foot in front of the other and suggests she holds the axe with two hands instead of one.

The woman hefts the axe over her head with both hands, biting her lip. She reels back, throws, and the axe doesn't even make it all the way to the bullseye. "Good try!" Scott says, reflexively, then starts correcting her posture.

The other two women near me are giggling as they watch. I can tell they're talking about Scott's good looks because they turn their backs toward me and whisper. More than once, Scott's gotten in trouble with our boss for sleeping with clients. It's too easy for him; he looks like the stereotypical jock and he's good at teaching. His gentle touch invites women—and a few men—to imagine what he'd be like in a different context.

In contrast, I wear glasses and have to practice every lesson in advance so I don't stumble over my words trying to explain things. I read more than I talk, so I once mispronounced the word "superfluous" in front of an entire tour group because I'd never used it out loud.

Leaving the women to their whispering, I gesture the family group over to an empty stall to start explaining the mechanics to them. The dad interrupts me several times as I do, but it's fine. I read a book about the male need to assert dominance and how it's an evolutionary imperative for some people, something they struggle to overcome. The book made the point that our human ability to conquer that instinct showed the higher evolution of nature. This man still has more in common with the monkeys, so

I treat him that way, allowing him to get his show out of the way so things don't become aggressive. I'm not interested in a fight today, or in impressing the man's wife. We're all following our evolutionary imperatives here and mine is to do my job well.

Eventually, I get the family throwing well enough that I can step away and survey how the rest of our tour group is doing.

The group of women are taking turns. The two whisperers are mostly hitting somewhere around the edge of the target. The curvy woman who went first is the worst throw I've ever seen. Every axe either doesn't go far enough, doesn't stick where it lands, or hits the wall. Scott keeps trying to give her small tips, suggesting she follow through on her throw or step into her front foot, and I see her listen and try to implement them. Still, she keeps flubbing her throws. I've never seen someone fail to hit the target so consistently.

I can see on her face that she's not surprised. This is a woman used to fucking up. She keeps chatting with her friends and smiling, but I see her bite her lip every time she takes a turn.

She continues to take her turns. She's not giving up.

Still, she's definitely not enjoying this and I hate that. The whole point of these adventure tours, and the activities we meticulously plan for them, is to get people out of their comfort zone and trying something that surprises them—in good ways. Nobody has fun when an activity makes them feel incompetent, so my job and the job of every guide here is to ensure people achieve basic mastery.

Scott's trying, but I can tell he's getting frustrated with Mollie's inability to improve. He meets my eyes briefly when he turns away from adjusting her stance yet again and gives a tiny shake of his head. *Lost cause.*

Giving up on a client means a bad review later, so I gesture to him, flicking my thumb back and forth between my group and his to ask if he wants to trade. Scott nods and doesn't take long to tell the women "my buddy Hunter" is going to help them now. He claps me on the back when we trade places. I know what it means: "Good luck."

It's fine. A book I read once about stubborn students—it was meant for public high school teachers—taught me some of the environmental and cultural factors that can make people tough to teach and made me much more patient.

"How are we doing?" I ask the three women, introducing myself to them.

Like the rest of the group, they're out-of-towners; I suspect from a city. They likely came here for a quaint mountain retreat and signed up for the adventure tour to have something to talk about when they went back home.

The one who's struggling the most, Mollie, stands behind her two friends. One of them is tall and blonde and skinny; the other is tall and brunette with an undercut on the left side of her head, a design of triple X's over an ear full of hoops and studs. Mollie is petite and I bet she feels like the odd one out more often than she admits.

"We're not very good at this," says one woman.

"It's our first time, though," adds the other. "We're axe-throwing virgins."

They snicker together. From the smell of their breath and the empty cups on the table nearby, I'd say they're aware this place serves booze.

"Not any more, you're not," I tell them. They giggle more.

"I'm the worst at it," says Mollie. "I can't seem to make my body do what the other guide—Scott?—showed me."

"You're just making us look better," one of her friends says to her. "Somebody has to do it." That makes Mollie's role in this trio pretty clear.

Mollie shrugs and smiles, not quite meeting my eyes.

"Want to try again?" I ask. "Or are you ready to call it quits?"

She grimaces, and I realize I shouldn't have given her option two. "Why don't you watch me a few times?"

I show them my most basic throw, using two hands and going slow. I do that a few times, pointing out my stance, how my weight moves as I throw, and my follow-through.

"You make it look so easy," Mollie says.

"It's only easy once you have the muscle memory," I assure. "Until then, it's always really hard to do something new."

One of her friends snorts when I say "really hard" and whispers something to the other friend.

This is the worst part of these tours: being objectified by the single women who come looking for an escape from their so-called real life. They forget that, for me, this *is* real life. My job is safely leading newbies on the kind of adventures that will get their heart racing and get them talking to their friends. But I go home at night to a room I rent from my boss because everything else around here is too expensive, driven up in price by the very tourists I serve for a living. I have a life fitted in around my adventures that includes laundry and clipping my toenails. I don't get to escape from reality by working here.

Scott revels in the larger-than-life allure his job gives him. I wear it like a badly chosen suit on a white water river trip. I try to make it fit, yet I'm constantly uncomfortable. Maybe I chose the wrong career, but I feel more like this career chose me. I'm from here. I grew up doing this. There weren't a lot of other options besides moving away to the city and probably wearing a tie every work day—never a real consideration for me.

Mollie steps forward suddenly and reaches for the axe I've been throwing. "Can I try again?" she asks.

I realize she sensed my discomfort and is volunteering herself to cover for her friends. I wonder how often she does this. Mollie is clearly the peacemaker. The empathetic smoother who makes it easier for everyone else to be less sensitive.

"Do you want me to help you adjust your stance?" I ask, holding up both hands so she understands I'm asking if I can touch her.

She bites her lip and nods.

In her eyes, I see determination and doubt. She's going to try again, but she's pretty sure she's going to fail.

I put my hands on her hips and turn her body an inch so she's facing the target by three quarters. "Does it feel better when you step forward as you throw or when you stand still? Try it a few times without the axe," I direct.

Stepping back, I watch as she tries to repeat everything I showed her. I fix her stance a few times, trying to imprint the body memory for her. She smells like coconut and her hips are plump, my fingers dipping right into the flesh there. I rarely get this close to clients for this long, but Mollie takes several tries to start repeating the correct movement.

"It's better when I line up and stay still, so my aim doesn't change," she eventually decides.

"OK, let's try that. How about when you hold the axe with one hand or two? Sometimes when you throw with two hands, it makes it steadier, and sometimes it's too much force. Try holding the axe without throwing it, just feel it when you hold it over your head."

I correct her a few more times, telling her to hold the axe over her head and not behind it, and to not let the weight of the axe pull it to either side. She decides to try it one-handed.

"OK, remember you've got to keep your wrist stiff so the axe goes where you're throwing it," I tell her, ignoring the giggles over "stiff" from the other women, who have refilled their cups. I'm sure they have many lovely qualities that are not at the forefront during this activity. "You want to release at the top of the throw, not at the level you're trying to hit," I coach Mollie. "Keep your eyes on the target the whole time, don't watch the axe."

"This is a lot to remember," she murmurs. Her body is tensing up.

"Hey, it's just a game. Nothing to get too worried about. Axe-throwing is a good way to get some justifiable rage out, if you have any. And I hear rage is justifiable for most women." I'm trying to win a smile, and I get one.

"I don't have too much rage," she denies. "Maybe some."

"Alright, well, channel that into your throw." I grin at her. "Not too much rage, though. The perfect amount. OK, Mollie. Give it a few warm-up throws. You got this."

Stepping away from her, I gesture at her friends that they should be filming this. She's got it this time. To their credit, they both fumble to get out their cell phones quickly and start recording.

Mollie repeats the throwing sequence twice, mimicking everything I showed her, before she lets an axe fly. It hits the target, barely off the bullseye. She screams in excitement. It's the first time her axe has stuck to the wall.

Her friends shriek too, jumping up and down.

I hold up both hands to give Mollie double high-fives and she jumps into my arms instead, surprising me. I give her a celebratory hug, unable to prevent her soft breasts from pressing against my chest. It's nice. She fits there perfectly.

Shit, it's been too long since I touched a woman. Half a year, at least, since Jenna and I broke up when she quit the adventure center and left town. No—that was last season, so nearly a year ago.

Before I can get too inappropriate, Mollie jumps back like she realized she's hugging a stranger. She gives me a shy smile and then rejoins her friends to re-watch the moment on their phone screens.

In the next stall, Scott meets my eyes. He gives me a thumbs up and I grin. This is why I became an adventure guide, after all.

The satisfaction of teaching someone how to do something they thought they couldn't gets me through the less fun parts of my job.

And sweet hugs from pretty women don't hurt, either, despite my misgivings about being the object of a stranger's affection.

two

MOLLIE

"THAT GUY WAS DEFINITELY INTO YOU."

"Hunter," I remind Sophie. "His name was Hunter." And he was tall and had a man bun that made me think I might actually be into man buns—a sentence I never thought I'd think.

"I'm *saying,* Hunter was really into you. You should go for it. Have a vacation fling."

Nora laughs. "That would be so out of character for Mollie!"

"Exactly why she should do it!" Sophie insists. "Get out of your rut, Mollie!"

I wish my friends would stop talking about my *rut.* I don't want everyone in this bar to know about my comfortable existence in which nothing extraordinary happens to me. Sophie recently got engaged and Nora got a promotion that shot her into the rarified air of six-figure salaries, so their energy is that of astronauts about to launch into space. I'm here to see them off on their journeys. And then wait for trip reports, like the little wife waiting at home.

That's nothing new; my own mother raised me on phone

calls home from her high-powered job. A single woman climbing the journalism career ladder needed a quiet child who didn't mind babysitting herself—finishing homework, making microwave dinners, putting herself to bed—as soon as she was old enough.

Sighing, I take another drink. My life isn't so bad, but it has a different definition of *exciting*. I mean, I almost cried when I saw the free dish of peanuts on our table when we sat down at this bar. Bars in the city where I live never offer free stuff.

Still, if exciting is this trip Nora and Sophie planned—forcing me to throw axes and ride bikes and hike into the woods and whatever else we're doing—maybe I'm OK without it. Today had been embarrassing. I was so bad at *throwing* things. I couldn't make my body do what my brain commanded. Even when Hunter patiently explained, repeatedly.

Nora and Sophie have moved on to talking about Sophie's wedding plans. I'm so excited for her. Her fiancé, Chad—despite his stereotypical "bro" name—is good to her and respectful of her friends. When I see him, he always remembers to ask about something I'd mentioned during the last visit. In my life, that's usually something dumb like the work baby shower I'm dreading or a new coworker I'm training even though they're higher up the chain of administrative power at my law firm than I am.

Chad and Sophie got engaged on a trip to Hawaii, so Sophie's having a hard time picking a honeymoon location. It's hard to hate Sophie, even though her problems are one-percenter issues. She's constantly terrified her good fortune will disappear and has been in therapy for anxiety since high school, when we first met.

Nora is the one who pushed Sophie to go to therapy in the first place. Nora, who says things like "let's take the emotion out of this and analyze it logically," has never found a problem without a solution—usually one she comes up with. Using an opened napkin on our tiny high-top table at this bar, she's now mapping out a spreadsheet for Sophie to select the perfect honeymoon location based on factors like weather, difficulty traveling, available activities, and "memorability."

If I were picking, I'd come here for a honeymoon. God, it's gorgeous here. We rode an actual gondola to get to this bar—a 12-minute ride up the mountain and to this adorable village that I bet is a snowy delight at Christmas time. It's a planned community, all the buildings matching each other and mostly hotels, restaurants, and vacation rentals. I can't deny the perfection of the facade. The mountains in this part of the state are startlingly close, jagged because they're the newest range in Colorado—as I read on a sign when we left the gondola—and still lightly dusted with snow despite being the middle of summer. This little town nestled in the middle of them couldn't be more idyllic.

At least my friends are distracted from convincing me to "go for it" with Hunter, the hot guide with the kind blue eyes behind glasses who managed to teach me how to throw an axe. I hit the target one time and stopped there, not wanting to ruin the high of my success with another dozen bad throws. He'd been so kind to me, like maybe he wasn't going to go home after and make fun of the incompetent girl with his other guide friends. *Maybe.*

The idea of Hunter making fun of me after being so kind makes me slump in my seat.

"Mollie, I've decided to make it my mission this week to get you more excited about life again," Nora says.

Uh oh. I've seen Nora on a mission many times. She doesn't give up. I admire her so much, with her daring haircuts and intense focus on everything she does. And she also scares me.

"I'm not *not* excited about life," I protest, lying. My two best friends since high school stare back at me, holding their beers and saying nothing.

"OK, well, sometimes life isn't that exciting and that's OK. Sometimes you've got to just…be a good human and try to get a good annual review at work."

I'd recently gotten my annual review at work. I got "meets expectations" across the board. Even my job thinks I'm boring.

"But not this week," Nora insists. "This week, you get excitement. It's your last hurrah before you turn 30. You're going to try biking and hiking and white-water rafting and you're going to kiss a stranger."

Cringe. None of that sounds like me. "I am?"

"Mollie!" Nora makes a face at me. "You have the agenda."

I do; Nora color-coded it. "Kissing a stranger definitely wasn't on there," I say, and press on before Nora promises to find a slot for it on our week-long schedule. "I just want to hang out with you guys. We never get to hang out like this anymore."

Nora and Sophie both reach out and grab my hands, then link hands with each other so we make a circle around the little table like we're about to pray, even though none of us is religious. "I know; I miss you guys so much," Sophie says. Sophie is moving out of state with Chad. Nora is always busy. I'm the one with all the free time that I spend, mostly, on my couch binge-watching every rom-com show that The Powers That Be grace us with. I talk to my mom a lot on the phone. I love my mom, but she's addicted to being the boss—the person people come to for answers—and it keeps her busy. Even though we live in the same city, we rarely meet up in person.

"And I'm so excited we're doing this friend-moon before our lives get even more crazy," Nora agrees, graciously including me in the craziness. There are no big changes on *my* horizon. "But this trip is really for Mollie. Don't you agree, Sophie?"

Sophie nods, her pretty face earnest. "Yes. Mollie, we worry about you. You haven't found your *thing*."

"My *thing*?" I repeat. Nothing about this trip is *for* me. I would have picked a relaxing beach, I think, not an "adventure" trip.

"Yes, your passion," Nora agrees. "The passion that gets you up in the mornings."

Briefly, I think about how many times I hit the snooze button during the week. How do my high school friends still know me so well when we've barely seen each other for the past few years? "I do OK," I protest, even though a voice in my own head—*traitor*—tells me, *the lady doth protest too much.* "Anyway, I don't think axe-throwing is my *thing*."

Sophie and Nora exchange a look. They both know I was terrible at it. "Well, no," Sophie agrees diplomatically. "That's why you've got to keep trying things until you find something that is!"

Good God, they're really going to force me to stay out of my comfort zone all week. The back of my neck starts to sweat. I'd signed onto this week of "adventure" to spend time with the friends I never see anymore. I have the best intentions to try everything on the agenda Nora and Sophie signed us up for. I'd even tried training for the mountain biking at that horrible spin class! I had also figured I could bail on any activities that terrified me. I don't want to be trapped into doing everything Sophie and Nora do; they're *much* more adventurous people than me. I mean, look at Nora's hair! "Um," I say weakly. "You really don't have to worry about me."

"We're your friends, we're always going to want better things for you," Sophie says, a weird turn of phrase that makes me suspect they've been having conversations behind my back where they pass judgment on my life. I have friends with less accomplished lives—friends who live for long Sunday brunches and cheap finds in the latest clothing trend—and they've never pushed me to look for "better." What's better than a bottomless mimosa?

OK, mimosas are actually the worst. All that sugar gives me an instant hangover. And I constantly have to deal with the nail-biting terror that is parallel parking when I go out to restaurants in the city.

Still, I go to brunch with my friends and try to ignore the painful boringness of my life; why can't Sophie and Nora? Maybe their lives *aren't* boring. Maybe I'm the only one.

Maybe we need more alcohol. I scan the bar for our waitress.

"Starting tomorrow, you should make a resolution to try every new thing you can while we're here," Nora announces, with the finality of a decision made for me. "By the end of the week, I bet you'll have found your thing. Or your thing can be *trying new things*! Maybe that's it!"

I blink at my friend. "Trying new things is not my thing. I hate trying new things."

"*Do* you?" Nora asks, like it's a serious question. "Are you *sure*?"

"Yeah, Mollie, how often have you tried new things?" Sophie chimes in. "It might be better than you expect. Especially with that hot guide there to *instruct* you." She and Nora exchange grins.

"You guys," I say, because despite my sweaty palms, I need to stop this disaster before it happens. "Hunter was just being nice while doing his job. Let's stop objectifying him."

"You're so sweet, Mollie," Nora sighs. "Always seeing the best in people while missing the opportunity they represent. Maybe *that's* your thing. Hunter probably *is* a nice guy. That's why we want you to sleep with him. He won't screw you and then pretend not to know you the rest of the week."

"I mean, he could still be like that," Sophie warns. "It's hard to tell with guys."

"Well, start with kissing, then," Nora replies, with surreal logic. "We'll work up to trusting him with plowing Mollie all night long."

"Shhh!" The tips of my ears are burning as I dart my gaze around the bar to see if anyone's listening. What if Hunter were *here*—not outside the realm of possibility, in a community this small—and heard that?

"Good idea, or they could wait until the night before we fly out and that way he won't get a chance to be a douchebag afterward," Sophie says. "Even if he wants to."

"Smart," Nora nods.

They both laugh at me for cowering into the smallest size I can on my side of the table.

"Mollie. You need to be fucked so bad," Sophie says. "How long has it been?"

"Oh my god," I say. "I don't keep track." That's a lie, of course.

"That's a lie," Nora says. "Every woman keeps track. I bet the time you're thinking of isn't even the last person you slept with. Getting fucked is different from having sex."

Whimpering, I put my head down on the table. The thing about Nora is, she's almost never wrong. The last time I "got fucked" was a disaster—he left after and unmatched me on the dating app—*and* it was the best sex I'd ever had. It was a year ago. I'd slept with guys since, but none were as memorable. Once, I'd been so drunk I cried, and he told me I should talk to a therapist while putting on his pants.

"I don't want to have a one-night-stand," I tell my friends. "They make me feel like shit."

"Well, it's important to know your boundaries," Nora agrees. I knew that would get her. Nora can't resist therapy-talk.

"Maybe only the make-out session, then," Sophie concedes. "You know we're not going to leave you alone until you agree to try something new. Something you wouldn't do back home."

And then they start discussing strategies to get me alone with Hunter over the next week we're here. Maybe we can invite him out for drinks (Sophie's idea) or lock the two of us in the equipment shed together (Nora's idea, assuming there is an equipment shed somewhere since we haven't seen the adventure center yet).

Poor Hunter, probably the inspiration behind many a city girl's plots to "have an adventure." How could he not be? The combination of that man bun with the glasses is like a nerdy He-Man. A gal desperately wants to take the glasses off and comb her hands through his blond hair. Or maybe I've had too much to drink that I'm imagining that, shifting against the crease in my jeans in the middle of a crowded public bar.

Another beer in, I find myself agreeing to their wild plots. I want them to stop trying to *convince* me. Yes, I need to get fucked, I find myself agreeing. Yes, Hunter is hot. Therefore, yes, I should get fucked by Hunter. Logic!

It's fine. I can bail on this plan later.

It's not like Hunter would be interested in me, anyway. He must have his pick of women—both local and out-of-towners. He's not at home thinking about me.

As though I splashed cold water down my front, I suddenly pull up short. My friends got me carried away with this fantasy, even though Hunter is a real person and not a tour we can sign up for. The "get fucked" tour. It's not like me to get lost in my thoughts to this extent, mixing up reality and what will never be.

What if Nora and Sophie are so determined to make it happen, they don't let go of this plan even when we sober up?

I agreed to come on what Nora said would be "the most memorable girls trip ever" because I miss my friends. I just didn't realize this trip was going to be memorable for the wrong reasons.

three

HUNTER

MY BOSS, Tom, is juggling a box of pastries and a folder of waivers for the tour. I'm not sure why he thought the two of us could handle pick-up alone. As usual, I volunteered before I thought twice. I'm Tom's go-to guy and I want it to stay that way. One of these days, maybe he'll notice and...what? Pat me on the back and offer me more money plus benefits? Any of that would be nice.

Tom's attitude, I guess, has something to do with the overly macho attitude of most of the guys I work with. Never ask one of these dudes "can you do it?" The answer is always yes. Even when it isn't.

"Can you hold these?" Tom passes over the folder. I smooth it out.

"Roger added some tiny line in there, I don't even know what, but said they looked good. Ironclad."

Roger Smith, the only lawyer in town, is over 70 and started practicing law in Telluride after retiring from some firm in Denver. I doubt how on top of things he remains, but I don't say anything. Both because he's sitting in the corner of this coffee shop and I don't particularly want to drive upstate to some expensive lawyer who might produce the same thing. If people get hurt on our trips, we've got bigger problems.

"You two got all that?" Even Dorothy, the coffee shop owner, looks skeptical. She's passing over the coffee thermos box and a bag of cups, sugar packets, and stirring sticks.

"We've got it, right, Hunter?" says my boss, who will never ask for help. I nod in loyal agreement, but give Dorothy a doubtful look.

"Do you want me to carry something? I'm going that way, anyway."

We turn and there's Mollie, the woman who struggled the most with axe throwing last night. We deliberately set up this morning's activities to start late because we knew most people would be out late celebrating the start of their tour-slash-vacation, but Mollie looks awake and clear-eyed. She's wearing some kind of lip gloss that shines under the coffee shop lights.

When I meet her eyes, her cheeks fill with color and she looks away.

"Don't worry about us!" Tom says cheerfully, as he balances a paper bag on top of a pastry box and the folder of important papers. He nods at me to get the two thermos boxes of coffee. "We're actually bringing this to the group. Figured everyone would need a little wake 'em up before we get started today."

"Do you want something to drink, dear?" Dorothy asks Mollie. There's a line out the door, but Dorothy will never let a customer leave thirsty.

"Oh, I'll just have some of what they're bringing to the group," Mollie demurs.

"Well, take one of these at least!" Dorothy pulls a mini muffin out of the case and hands it to Mollie in a napkin. Mollie reaches for her purse. Dorothy waves her off. "You'll come back after you try that, I'm not worried!"

Mollie turns to walk with us. "That was so nice," she says when we get out to the sidewalk, looking stunned. She lifts the muffin to her mouth and I watch her take a bite. She's like a magnet for my eyes.

"Dorothy's a savvy lady," Tom says. "First bite's free, then you'll be hooked for life!"

"This *is* really good," Molly agrees, covering her mouth with one hand as she chews. We start down the side of the street in the direction of the adventure center.

"That'll have you ready for action!" Tom says cheerfully. Tom is a man who speaks in exclamation points, a very real stereotype of an outdoorsy man who's used to working with his hands and shouting over great distances. Every time he catches me reading in the main room at the house where we all live—we're his renters as well as his employees—he gives me a look like I'm masturbating in public. Maybe that's because, the last time I showed him an interesting line in a book I was reading, he protested that it was all blurry. I've been trying to convince him to get reading glasses ever since. I guess they're not manly enough for him.

"The agenda said today is a prep day?" Mollie looks worried.

"That's right," Tom agrees. "Rather than have everybody buy their own gear, we're loaning you used stuff. That means everyone needs to get fitted. And then...well, I'll let Hunter tell you about it. This whole tour is his idea."

"Really?" Mollie turns her focus on me. Her eyes tell me she's tuned in to my answer, not the distractions of blue sky and fresh air or all the people we're passing as we walk down the street toward the adventure center on the edge of town.

Since she actually looks interested, I give her a real answer. "I read a book about the subscription model that included a lot about packaging products together. I thought, why wouldn't that work for experiences, too?"

"He's on me to launch a membership model, too," Tom adds, chuckling. To his credit, Tom listens to my ideas—sure, he laughs at them, calling them "modern," then eventually tries them and they work.

This morning, I'd suggested upgrading our bookkeeping method to a program that tracks all the accounts in one place. He'd shuddered dramatically and said he didn't want any outside company to have all his information. Last year, I'd convinced Tom to move from paper to a computer spreadsheet, so I figured it was time to make another recommendation. Baby steps.

"I think that's really smart," Mollie says softly. She has a voice that makes me lean in to hear her, like she's not used to people listening.

"So what brought you to the adventure tour?" I ask.

She laughs softly, almost under her breath. "I wanted to be more adventurous, I guess."

The people who visit our town specifically to "have adventures" tend to be looking for adrenaline. They want to ride that high that comes from speed and a little danger. I don't get that vibe from Mollie.

"What's something adventurous you've done in the last year?" I ask her, softly enough that Tom, who is greeting people we pass, might not hear.

She looks at me like I've asked her what color her underwear is.

"Anything," I prompt gently. "The first thing that comes to mind."

"I drove down to visit a hot spring in New Mexico by myself last month," she says, after a long moment in which I'm not sure she'll answer me. "I'm scouting out locations for Sophie's bridal shower."

Mollie clicks into place for me. She does things for others, not herself. Like this tour. She's clearly here for her friends.

"Anything you're looking forward to on this tour?" I ask.

"This prep day," she admits, looking down at the coffee and not at me. "I'm really glad we're going to learn more about what we're doing before we do it."

"I'm glad you feel that way, because I think a lot of people are going to skip it. At least I'll have one eager student."

"Skip it?" She looks bewildered. "But why?"

Before I can explain about the lack of adrenaline, Tom is hurrying us along as if we were the ones pausing to talk to everyone we passed.

In the lobby of the adventure center, less than a dozen people are slouched on our collection of pre-loved furniture sourced from garage sales and donations. They include the family I taught last night, three 20-something men I'd quickly labeled the Trouble Trio, the skinny teenage boy from another family—apparently here on his own—and Mollie. Two other guides have shown up, as required, but Scott is nowhere to be seen. Scott is Tom's real favorite, so he can get away with this.

We pass around coffee, Mollie helping with the organization by setting out cups for me to pour.

I stay close to her, wanting to ensure she has a good experience. She's curvy, and it's important that she be fitted for a bag that sits at her hips, not where it will chafe and make her uncomfortable. My hope is always that people will walk away from these trips with a newfound hobby that they keep doing. Pain is a deterrent to that goal.

Plus, there's something about Mollie that tells me she needs a fun experience—and doesn't expect it. She's gritting her teeth through this tour. But I designed it to speak to people's souls and I know it can do that for her, too.

She listens intently to my spiel about safety, staying on trails, and speaking up about raw skin, which can form blisters that become difficult to deal with on the trail. We've only scheduled a one-night backpacking trip for this tour—all activities were planned with beginners in mind—but I don't want a night ruined dealing with first aid that could have been prevented.

I sidle up to her after, when a few people are getting that second cup of coffee, and let her in on the secret: "I'll be repeating all that later, probably more than once, for the benefit of people who weren't here or forgot everything."

"Oh, of course," she says, tucking away the phone I saw her clearly using to take notes.

"Are you nervous?"

"No! Well, yes. But this isn't as scary as..." She catches herself. "Some things."

Now I'm concerned. Mollie is already struggling; if this isn't the worst of it, I'd better find out what is. "What part of the trip are you most nervous about?"

She shakes her head and bites her lip, one plump bit of flesh turning white. I want to lecture her about raw skin again, watching this. I manage to hold it in.

"If you tell me, I may be able to help," I shamelessly wheedle.

She smiles a little and I can tell I've got her. Mollie is the kind of person who hates to disappoint you, and I feel a little bad for taking advantage of that.

"The mountain biking," she admits. "After we signed up, I started getting all these videos of crashes on my social feed."

"Ah." I nod. I'm not on social media, but I've seen some pretty gnarly real-life crashes in my time. Scott nearly broke his arm last week on a rock feature. "I won't make you do anything technical. Or anything you don't want to try. I'm here to help make trying something new safe for you."

One of the 20-something dudes standing nearby decides to intervene for no reason. "That's the whole point of these guys, to keep us idiots from doing something idiotic."

Nodding along, I step back to let our circle grow. I immediately miss speaking one-to-one with Mollie. Still, half the point of these tours is to foster friendship. Among the participants, *not* between them and the tour guides. We're here to smooth the way, not be part of the adventure. Despite Scott's best efforts.

It's never been this difficult to remind myself of that reality.

The other two guys from the Trouble Trio overtake the circle a bit, nudging me to the outside as they home in on Mollie. I watch her, looking overwhelmed but nice about it.

"These tour guides know more about the outdoors than anything else," one of them says, like I'm not standing right there.

Mollie meets my eyes. "I guess I should be listening to them, then," she says, a mild rebuke the others ignore.

My first instinct is to save her, but I'm projecting. I *want* her to need my protection. Maybe she likes the attention. I raise my eyebrows at her and she smiles back, so I step away.

I get this a lot from tourists. They trust me to keep them safe on the trails, and still assume I can't read or write or do arithmetic. I have a college degree. Sure, it's an associate that I got in two years commuting to Montrose—long days of sitting in the car, one of my least favorite things. That's not nothing. In reality, I could have done something else, but if it involves sitting in an office for eight hours at a time, no thanks.

I'd rather put up with a few ignorant assholes who think I'm limited to being "trail smart" and nothing more.

MOLLIE

I'M GOING *to get so wet.*

Staring at Hunter, who is shirtless and balancing with loose limbs on his paddleboard in front of me, I ignore the teasing whispers of my friends. They're still stuck on the possibility I could have a "vacation fling" with him and his current appearance is not stemming the tide.

What I'm more worried about is my complete lack of balance.

I'm kneeling on my paddleboard while everyone around me stands. The three guys I met this morning are even waving their paddles at each other in a mock sword fight.

Even in this position, I'm wobbling. I'm the person who can't hold tree pose for more than a second in yoga. It doesn't matter how hard I stare at a spot on the wall or "soften my gaze" or whatever instructors have told me to try; the truth is, I'm an unbalanced person and always will be.

This water doesn't look too bad. I can't see the bottom of the lake we're on, but I can see at least a foot under the surface. There's nothing scary in here. It'll be fine when I fall over.

"Try standing," one of the instructors—not Hunter—encourages me. "You can get a lot more power in your stroke if you stand."

"Try it for a minute," Nora urges. She and Sophie are standing on their boards nearby, looking lithe and sporty in their swimsuits. Their life vests don't even look that bulky on them. I'm wearing shorts and a sunshirt because I don't want to a) get sunburnt, or b) flash my ass at everyone here while I flail around on this board. I *told* them I hate trying new things. It's because I'm so bad at everything at first.

It's clear that they're not going to let me get away with not even trying. Still, I wait until some of the other people in the group have sped away in all directions across the lake so fewer people see me. My legs are trembling as I carefully stand, one leg after another. I almost freeze when I have one leg in front of me, but Nora and Sophie are watching. It feels so high up here, like I'm standing on water. My brain screams, *Unnatural!* I hope no one can see how badly I'm shaking, half hunched over so my chest is parallel to the board.

Now I need to pick up my paddle and slowly...carefully... straighten up.

It happens then, I slip. I throw my arms out to both sides, knowing there's nothing to catch myself on and I'm definitely going in.

"Whoa!" Someone catches my right hand and holds as steady as a rock. I don't fall. I look over at Hunter, who is floating on his board next to me looking serious.

"Plant your feet a little wider on the board," he tells me, his voice calm and firm. I do as he tells me. "And don't lock your knees. That's right."

My butt is sticking out behind me, I'm bending my knees so much. I'm basically doing squats on this board and must look ridiculous.

"Now shuffle back on the board a few inches. You should be standing just behind the center line."

"Are you sure?" I squeak. Despite all evidence of its stability, I'm worried about the board flying out from between my legs.

"I'm sure," he says, still holding my hand. I shuffle back until I'm doing my squat on the back half of the board.

"There you go. This is the position you should keep while you paddle. Can you remember that?"

My thighs are burning. What are they going to torture me with next? I nod mechanically. "Got it."

"You can kneel to paddle," Hunter says gently. "There's nothing wrong with it. No wrong way to get some exercise if you're having fun. Try it."

I cling to Hunter until I'm back on my knees on the board.

"Try sitting," he suggests. I don't look up at him, because the sun is behind him, but I obey his instructions. When I sit with my legs crossed, I stop shaking. I try an experimental paddle, stroking it through the water at my side. I don't move much—and that's OK because I like going slow. It's safer.

"There you go!" Hunter sounds much more excited for me than this warrants. "Fun, right?"

Looking back at him, I smile. "I can do this."

"Great. Keep at it," he tells me. "And later when you jump in, you can do it on your terms."

Laughing too loudly out of relief, my heart rate slowly settles back to a normal speed. Now I can appreciate the gorgeous setting we're in, a lake surrounded by slopes of evergreen that go vertical, leaping out of the ground to attack the sky in mountain shape. We're only a few miles from town, and still it feels like we're deep in nature. The cold water is still, the sky is blue. A postcard couldn't be more beautiful.

Sticking close to shore, I paddle around like that for a while, watching as everyone else disappears. Nora and Sophie are racing each other across the lake. The three guys around our age start chasing them, coming from far across the water. Everyone is going much faster and farther than me.

I sort of want to try to stand up again, but I'm worried it will be another disaster.

Hunter keeps circling back to check on me. I watch him glide across the water toward the island in the center of the lake, stop to talk to the family resting on their boards as they float on the surface, then head back my way.

My eyes fill with tears of self-pity. Hunter's so patient to babysit me. He must hate it. How could he not?

He stops paddling once he's close enough to talk to me. He doesn't say anything. He puts his paddle across the front of his board and sits down astride it, legs hanging in the water on either side. We sit, drifting on the mild waves, Hunter watching what we can see of the rest of the group and me watching Hunter. I can't help it. The man is shirtless and his muscles are like a movie star's. Except, I bet he comes by them naturally, not from a gym.

"Aren't you going to burn?" I blurt out, my brain apparently stunned by the sheer expanse of bare skin.

Hunter looks over his shoulder at me. He grins. "I've lived here my whole life. I'm doing OK. But you know, maybe to be safe..." And then he slips over the side of his board into the water.

Hunter and I could almost be alone here, with everyone else far across the lake. We've drifted from shore a little to where it's deep enough that Hunter probably can't touch the bottom. His head rises back above the surface. He holds onto his board while he throws his head back and runs his hand over his hair like a wet dream.

Am I actually asleep right now? What would a bolder, dream-Mollie do?

"Don't give me ideas," I try, experimentally flirting. My cheeks immediately feel hot, but maybe that's the sun.

Hunter looks up at me, smiling. "I'm trying. Really pulling out all the stops here, Mollie."

My heart flutters a little. *Is he flirting back?* "Why?"

"I want you to have fun on this trip."

"I'm having fun," I protest. I watch the muscles in his shoulders flex as he keeps his hold on the board, floating off the side. Don't get this view in the city much.

"Are you?" he challenges me. "Would anything make this *more* fun?"

Being better at this would be more fun. I don't want to say that, because it might make Hunter encourage me to try again. While trying to think about it, I wipe the sweat off the top of my lip. I dip my other hand in the cool water.

"It's nice in here," he coaxes.

I pull off my shirt, exposing my shoulders and bikini-clad breasts to the sun, and slide into the water. I don't go all the way under, holding tight to my board so I don't lose it.

Hunter splashes me gently. "There you go. Living in the moment. Making memories. How's that feel?"

I splash him back. "Shut up. You don't have to babysit me, you know."

"I'm not babysitting you. I'm having fun, too."

I'm skeptical and give him a look that says so.

"Why do you think it's so hard to be here with you?" Hunter raises one arm and gestures around us. "Look at this. It's great, isn't it?"

Looking around, I take in the scene. The gentle lap of the

water against the board under my arm. The green trees lining the shore. The sun beating down from a cloudless blue sky. This man, insisting he's enjoying himself. And having nothing better to do with my time. "OK, you have a point."

He laughs. "Thank you."

"I'm sorry, I've always been a worrier." I'm embarrassed to admit this to someone like him, someone who seems to live his life to the absolute fullest.

"Better than never planning for what could go wrong."

"Is it?"

"In my line of business, it is."

I smile at him across my board and he smiles back across his. It's suddenly like we're sitting across from each other on a first date. Making small talk and learning each other's body language. *Shit.* I want that to be true so badly it takes my breath away.

"What are you worried about right now?" he asks.

And I can't tell him the truth, so I say, "That a water snake is going to slither up my pants." It's not *un*true.

Hunter throws back his head and laughs. "Don't worry, I'd pull it out if it did."

"You're supposed to say there are no water snakes in this lake!" I conveniently ignore the mental image of Hunter sticking his hands down my pants. Was that flutter in my shorts from him or an actual creature floating around this lake? I decide to hoist myself back up on my board. It takes a few tries.

"Need a boost?" Hunter circles under his board and holds out his hand when I'm mid-way out of the water.

"Maybe," I huff, clinging to my board with both arms and hoping it doesn't flip. The next thing I feel is Hunter's hand on my ass, shoving me up and onto the board. That time the flutter was definitely not a water snake.

Sitting with the board between my legs, I watch Hunter easily climb back onto his and try not to imagine what this metaphor would lead to if we were on a real date. Then he throws another smile over his shoulder at me and says, "Back to work."

As he paddles away and Nora and Sophie show up to tease me about having a "moment" with my "fling," I cling to the reminder about having fun. Because Hunter distracted me from my worries long enough for me to realize, I am.

five

HUNTER

I DON'T GO OUT with the guys very often—I'd rather be reading a book at home with my beer on the side table—and when I do, we usually go to one of the bars in town that mostly locals frequent. Tonight, we're at The Bivy, located in the tourist trap part of town up the mountain.

"What are we doing here?" I grumble to Scott as we're walking in. Most of the guides are here, another reason I decided to come. One of the benefits of *not* being in charge at the adventure center is I get to be "just one of the guys." I try to fit in, even if it means hiding my nerdy tendencies once in a while.

"Some of the girls suggested it," replies Scott, who knows all about my nerdy and rule-following tendencies, which is why he didn't tell me we were meeting up with some of the tour participants.

Of course. I catch sight of them now—there's Mollie, Nora, and Sophie, a mom who appears to have left her family at the hotel, and a definitely underage teen girl I'll have to keep an eye on. They're all parked at a large table near the pool tables and wave their drinks at us as we come in.

Scott approaches the table fast and I notice he acknowledges Mollie and Nora first, putting a hand on both of their shoulders as he greets everyone else. *Isn't Nora engaged? Or is that the other one.* I do a quick ring check and see that he has, at least, restrained his impulses enough to stick with the unattached women.

Biting off a sigh, I offer to get drinks for the table to hide how judgy I'm being. Scott's a great guide, firm but kind about dangers and guidelines. He's the same way in his personal life, laying out clear boundaries for the guys. Commenting on his rich and varied love life is a hard line and it's not my business, anyway. Hopefully, he's as clear about expectations with the women in his life. What do I care if he pursues Nora or Mollie or anyone else? Other than the fact that fraternization between guides and tour guests is against the rules. I've pointed this out before, and Scott laughed and said, "We're not doing rocket science here." He'd said it in front of Tom, who laughed with him.

Tom doesn't run things the way I would, but he's the boss and it's working for him, so I try to shut up about things like rule-following.

I nod at Mollie across the table as I sit down. She smiles back shyly. The last time I saw her, she was soaking wet, every curve on her body outlined in a clingy fabric. Tonight, she's wearing jeans and a drapey shirt that dips down to the tops of her breasts. Her short hair and dangling earrings draw attention to the exposed skin of her long neck.

She and Nora are polar opposites, sitting next to each other. I can't predict which one Scott will go after—hell, knowing Scott, maybe he'll convince them to share.

The idea makes me uncomfortable. Scott always tells me I

miss out on life by following all the rules, and I tell him I'll live a longer one because of it. We get along because we can agree to disagree on life philosophies.

Still, at the moment I wish I could channel some Scott and be less awkward. "How's your beer?" I ask Mollie. She's clutching a half-full pint glass.

"Good," she replies, nodding. Then she scrunches up her nose and shakes her head. "I mean, I don't like it."

"Do you want me to get you something different? Maybe a cocktail?" I shout it over the loud bar.

Sophie, talking to Tyler, one of the other guides, shouts at Mollie, "Why don't you move to the other side?" There's an empty chair beside me.

Nora leans over to Mollie and I see her lips sound out what is very clearly the words, "Go get him."

They're going to be disappointed in the evening. Tom will never trust me to help run the business if I start breaking the rules. Chatting at a bar is one thing, and bringing a guest back to the house I live in *with* my boss is another.

The back of my neck feels hot as I imagine bringing Mollie to my room, though. What would she think of the tidy bookshelves lining the walls around my bed? "You haven't left room for anything kinky," Scott said when he saw what I'd built last summer.

This guy lives in my head rent free sometimes, reminding me what I'm not.

Mollie sits down on the chair beside me and smiles like she doesn't mind that I'm not Scott.

"Hi...how's your trip going?" I know I'm an awkward conversationalist, better when I'm teaching or learning. I read a book once about how to make friends and it basically said to keep asking questions.

"Well, I know how to wear a backpack now." She actually

seems enthused about this, not throwing me an awkward bone. "I've never even used those waist strap thingies."

"That will completely change the way you look at a back-pack! You'll have much less discomfort if we got the fitting right."

"I'm sure you did." She lifts her beer at me. "You took your time on it."

"Oh, don't drink that! I was going to get you something different." I jump up and rush to the bar to get away from my embarrassment that she noticed the other day how carefully I adjusted every backpack to find the right fit. I enjoyed it far more than I normally would as I jerked on loose straps that made her jiggle in interesting places.

The bar is busy, filled with tourists who mostly have the benefit of staying within walking distance at one of the many hotels nearby. People are getting louder as they drink.

My friend Valentine works at The Bivy, and when it's slow, she will describe the steps to making cocktails and show me her work. She's here tonight, but running back and forth behind the bar. "Think you can get me something touristy when you've got a chance?" I call out to her.

She makes a face. "What do you think I do *all* day? Can you be more specific?"

Making an educated guess, I give her a taste profile. She raises her eyebrows, so I know there will questions when she has more time, but nods.

"I figured at least one of these would suit you," I tell Mollie when I get back to the table and set a whiskey sour and a vodka mule in front of her. "Sweet and sour or sweet and spicy?"

She bites her lip, trying to hide a delighted smile. "What's your guess?"

Pushing the vodka mule toward her, I watch her face.

"Really? You think I'm spicy?" She blushes and takes the drink. "Most people wouldn't."

"Guess they're not looking closely enough," I reply, taking a sip of the other drink.

She laughs. "Count me among them."

"Daring might be the better word. Sweet and daring. You're here on this tour, aren't you?"

"I hate to tell you this but this trip was not my idea. It was Nora's."

"You still said yes. And I get it, maybe you only wanted to spend time with your friends, but I've been watching you. You attack every activity like it's your job. I bet you studied or practiced before you got here, too."

Mollie studies me, her pupils lit up from the neon sign on the wall behind me. "I read a book," she admits.

"You did? Which one?" I lean in, hoping it's one I've read. Maybe that's on my shelves at home.

"It was about people who survive big disasters, like getting lost in the wilderness, and what it takes. It scared the shit out of me." She lowers her voice when she says "shit," like we're surrounded by impressionable children instead of rowdy adults.

"I promise I won't let you get lost in the wilderness on this trip," I tell her seriously. "But did you learn anything?"

She smiles wryly. "I learned I probably don't have what it takes to survive something like that. So I'm depending on you here, Hunter."

It might be the first time she's said my name. That's how it lands with me, anyway. Like she plucked me out of a herd of other guides—all of us trail smart guys who "know more about the outdoors than anything else"—and saw something unique in me.

"Out of all of us, Hunter's the guy you want when you get lost in the wilderness," Scott pipes up, popping our bubble. I didn't realize he was listening. "This guy's certified in everything you can be certified in, practically. CPR, First Aid, AED, Mountaineering, Orienteering, Lifeguarding…"

"Shouldn't you all know how to do those things?" Nora asks skeptically.

Scott puts his arm around her and says, "There's knowing how and there's passing the test. Hunter's a test-taker. He even got his kinesiology degree."

We're veering into territory I don't want to get into here. I hate talking about the fact that I only have an associate degree from the community college. "It's more practical than a degree in theater," I retort.

"Who has a degree in theater?" Nora's eyes widen as she looks at Scott. "No!"

"It was my rebellious phase," he shrugs, trying to brush it off.

"What, were you in it for the chicks?"

I've successfully diverted Nora and Scott, at least. Mollie is still studying me, so I stand. "Be right back," I say, and head for the bathroom.

Valentine catches me on the way back, when we're both down the back hallway. "Look at you, out with the city folk," she teases. Valentine—another Telluride native—makes cool content for a short-video platform in her free time, so she has an eye for a narrative.

"It's nothing," I insist.

She pokes me in the chest. "I'm going to let you get away with that because I only have a few minutes to pee, but I'm watching you, Mr. Man Bun."

Rolling my eyes, I edge past her. "Haircuts are for people with a 401K," I inform her, my usual retort. She laughs, as usual, and flips the hair in a long braid over her shoulder. Poor people humor.

When I get back to the restaurant, the group has moved.

Nora and Scott are playing pool. Tyler and a couple of the other guides are playing darts. I look around for Sophie and Mollie, even walking outside to check the patio. I hear them before I see them.

"It's not like you have to marry him just because you sleep with him." That's Sophie. They're standing by the outside bar, probably waiting on drinks.

"I barely know him, Sophie." That's Mollie. I stand hesitating, barely outside their line of sight. Obviously, I shouldn't listen because what they talk about is none of my business, except something tells me they're talking about me.

"Girl, we have a week. Get to know his *body*."

"OK, *Nora*. I expect this from her, not you. You know I'm not good at one-night-stands. I want what you have: a relationship."

"A relationship is for real life, not vacation. A relationship happens when you live in the same place and have the same lifestyle. That is not what this is. This is trying new things and having a little fun. And maybe you go back to your real life and have a different perspective on reality."

"You think I need a different perspective on life?"

"I think you're not entirely happy with it, so getting turned upside down and slapped on the ass a few times couldn't hurt. That man looks like he could do some serious butt-slapping. I saw him with his shirt off today."

Standing there eavesdropping, my skin heats at the graphic descriptions.

"Sophie, oh my god."

"Mollie. I'm completely serious. I know you're committed to do everything on the agenda, so I'm telling you right now, I'm putting sex on the schedule. You have to do it now. Before the end of the trip."

"Sophie!"

"I don't care if it's with Hunter or Scott or one of the other guys. You *need* some sexual adventure. Admit I'm not wrong."

A pause, then Mollie's small voice: "You're not wrong."

Backing away from the conversation, I stay silent. So Mollie wants—or her friends want for her—a vacation fling. I've never done that. I'm a relationship guy, not a fling guy. Unlike Scott, I don't sleep with the tourists or the clients, in part because there's always a time limit.

If I were Scott, this would be the perfect set up. No commitments, clear end point, and a week of fun with a beautiful woman open to trying new things.

I imagine Mollie's face, the way she bites her lip when she's nervous and then goes for it despite her fears, stepping up to try something with that determined look on her face. Open to learn. Ready to practice.

Scott would be the perfect teacher in that context. I'd be terrible. I only teach when I've done enough studying and practicing on my own to feel I've mastered something. And I'll never be the master of casual vacation sex. It's not in me.

Imagining Scott and Mollie together—becoming *experts*—curdles the drink in my stomach. Either Mollie doesn't get the full experience she wants this week, or I need to master my feelings on this subject. And fast.

six

MOLLIE

IT'S MY WATERLOO. My Rubicon. The ruin of me. My point of no return.

My stomach is rejecting the muffin I bought at the coffee shop this morning—blueberry and lemon curd, it was *amazing*—and I might cry.

The bike between my legs feels totally unnatural. It has huge tires and a bunch of levers I don't understand on the handlebars. This bike means business. I have no *business* being on it.

"This is called sessioning," Hunter is saying. He's standing with his own bike in front of the group, gesturing out at the trail in front of us. "It means repeating something over and over until you master it. Trying again and again until you have a good feel for how to handle a feature or a problem. There is no shame in not being able to execute something the first time you try it. Sessioning is how you get better."

I need to session getting on this bike a few times more. Maybe for the rest of this class.

"We're going to ride a little way down this trail, which is

completely flat, to a clearing and then we're going to practice some techniques."

My legs are shaking. *They're just trembling, Mollie, don't be dramatic!* I'm going to embarrass myself in front of everyone, including Hunter.

Checking in on the phone last night, my mom told me I have to take some risks to "reach for your dreams." But what dream am I reaching for? I don't remember wanting to climb on a borrowed bike and risk life and limb on a trail covered with rocks the size of my head. Do I even have any dreams? At the moment, my mind is blank. This helmet is so heavy. I want to lay down in the dirt and pretend I'm not here.

Beside me, Nora and Sophie are setting up a group selfie and gesturing for me to join in. They look cute and adventurous in their helmets, in contrast to my hard-topped mushroom. Beneath it, my head itches.

Scott, the guide that I swear Nora has a crush on, wanders over and offers to take our picture.

"Get the bikes in!" Nora insists, handing him the camera. "Make us look hardcore."

"I don't have to try for that," Scott says with a flirty grin.

She laughs and swats his arm.

It's possible I'm dissociating. I can't feel my feet as Sophie and Nora wrap their arms around me and grin for the camera. Somehow, I ended up in the middle of the picture, like this is *my* idea.

"Does anybody have any questions before we head out?" Hunter calls to the group.

I should have questions. My brain is filled with shrieking instead. *Am I going to die out here?* Don't ask that.

OK, at the most you'll break a leg. Let's not jump to catastrophe, Mollie. The voice in my head sounds like my mother. Calm and rational. That voice is overruled by my terror over what I'm about to do.

My vision is like a tunnel as I watch my hands clasp my bike handles and throw a leg over the bike. Scott came over and bounced my bike up and down a few times earlier—a preview for what's going to happen when I go over those giant rocks, I guess. Nothing fell off or apart, so he called it good. What about me? Doesn't someone need to bounce me up and down a few times?

That's what she said. Even in my hyper state, I can't help giggling to myself silently. It has an edge of hysteria to it, even inside my head. My brain wants to veer off into any other topic besides the one at hand as I stare at what looks like a sharp drop-off to the side of this tiny little trail in front of me.

"Keep it loose," Scott says to me. I blink at him. He's sitting on his bike between me and Nora. I didn't even notice him there.

"What?"

"Don't lock your muscles. You want to move with the bike a little bit. We'll talk about when you move the bike under you versus moving with the bike, but for now, focus on not tensing up. You OK?"

No. Definitely not. *Omigod, can I say I'm sick and get out of this?* I swallow. I need to face my fear. So I have terrible balance and no mind-body control, or whatever it was Hunter called it. Half the time, my body does whatever it wants without checking in with my brain. That's the problem.

"I'm OK," I say faintly.

"Feel free to walk your bike at any point if you're uncomfortable trying something," he says. He looks serious, not realizing this sounds like permission to never get on my bike again. "And if you're not sure, ask me or Hunter to help you out."

"OK," I repeat, bobbing my head. Nora says something to Scott and he turns away from me. I'm like a child. *What do I want, training wheels?* I need to toughen up. I'm a city girl. I walk down streets every day more dangerous than this silly little trail.

And I hate every second of my morning commute in the city, too—dodging people on the walk from the parking complex to the office, waiting at street lights in a crowd of other miserable office workers, the women wearing shoes they clearly plan to change and the men looking at their watches every few seconds.

Closing my eyes, I take a deep breath. At least I don't smell car exhaust and perfume. We're out in another picture-perfect location, the trees blocking us from a view of the town that had taken my breath away on the way up. Telluride is gorgeous, nestled in a valley with a waterfall visible on one end.

When I open my eyes again, they land on Hunter. Standing at the front of the group demonstrating something on his bike, he's wearing funny padded shorts that make his butt look big and a zippered shirt that shows some chest hair. He's probably never worn dress shoes in his life. I'm jealous of that.

"Everybody ready?" he calls out. "OK, follow me! Scott will follow behind the group." And then he pedals his bike over the small ridge and disappears down the trail.

"This is going to be so fun!" Sophie squeals, following him.

"See you in a bit," Scott says to Nora, who follows Sophie.

Not letting myself stop to doubt more, I sit on my bike seat and follow. *It's just like riding a bike!* So far so good. I hold my breath when I go over the ridge, and then I don't even notice a drop. It was smaller than it looked. *Maybe this is going to be OK.*

An hour later, I'm staring at a sheer rock listening to Hunter describe how to ride up it. *This is not OK.*

They lulled me into complacency until now, with the riding in circles and along pretend switchbacks. All "only use one finger on the brake" and "put the pedal under the ball of your foot." Easy. We'd practiced body positioning, which I still don't quite get—"if the bike were to disappear, you should be standing on the ground" did not compute for me—and I managed to fake it well enough.

But I can't do this. I can't ride a bike up a rock.

I've already watched Nora and Sophie succeed on their first try. They make it look easy, even with the grunting (Nora) and squealing (Sophie) involved.

The words are on the tip of my tongue: "I'm going to walk it." They won't come out. I'm the last person in the group to go and no one else walked their bike. Hunter is standing uphill waiting and Scott is watching me from halfway up the slope.

"You good?" one of them calls to me. My throat is too tight to answer, so I answer with a thumbs up. *My thumb is such a liar.*

Between the sun beating down on me and the pressure of expectation on my back, my shoulders are hunched. My whole body is a knot of tension. I'm going to have to try to do this, no matter how scared I am that I'm going to screw it up. Nora and Sophie think I need to try new things to break out of the rut I'm in. Well, now I'm going to ride right up a rut and show it who's boss.

I repeat the instructions over and over in my head: *Lift the front wheel when you're about to hit the rock. Pedal through it. When you're about to leave the rock, shove the bike in front of you.*

Wait, how do I know I'm not lifting too early? And was I supposed to lean backward or forward?

It's too late to ask them to repeat the lesson. I pedal forward. When I'm about to hit the rock, I panic and hit the brakes. I guess I'm a little late on the timing because my front wheel sticks while my back wheel keeps going, and the bike tips over. I shriek even before I hit the ground and feel pain in my hands and knees. The bike falls on top of me, an afterthought since I wasn't going very fast.

My first reaction is embarrassment. Nobody else fell trying to do this. When I start to push myself to my feet, Scott stops me. "Lay there for a minute. Let it settle." He lifts the bike off my body, untangling it gently from my legs.

Hunter arrives next, having run down the hill I guess, and squats down next to me. "What are you feeling?" he asks.

"Dumb, mostly," I reply, squinting up at him in the sun.

He smiles a little. "I meant in your body. Where are you hurt?"

"Oh." I lift a hand and see it's bloody. "My hands. And my knees."

"Yeah, you've got some scrapes. Anywhere else?"

"Um, I don't think so." I carefully sit up. Hunter helps me examine my arms and legs for any other scrapes. Nothing seems broken.

Scott gives me a thumbs up and calls up to the rest of the group looking over the top of the hill, "We've got first blood!"

"I'll get you patched up," Hunter assures me. He's already pulled out a first aid kit. "You can take the rest of the group to the next feature," he tells Scott. "We'll catch up."

"OK, you got it," Scott says affably. "Hang in there, Mollie. It's all part of the action."

I mumble a curse under my breath and they both laugh at me.

"Mollie, do you want us to stay?" Nora calls down to me. She's holding onto her bike and looking worriedly back at Sophie.

"No, go ahead!" I call back. "I'm OK!" I throw a thumbs up their way for good measure, even though my eyes are filling with delayed tears. *This sucks.* I'm sick of faking it for my friends and everyone else, like I'm somehow enjoying being bad at things.

"OK, we'll see you in a little bit! Take good care of her, Hunter!" Sophie calls.

Hunter gives them another thumbs up before he goes back to unwrapping an antibacterial wipe. So many lying thumbs-ups.

Like a child waiting for their mother to make it better, I hold my hands out to him.

"I don't have any gloves," he tells me, offering me the wipe. "It might be better if you..."

"Oh, right," I say, taking the wipe and dabbing at my other hand with it. *What must he think of me?* Probably that only an idiot would get hurt on such a small—what did he call it? A "feature"? *I prefer my ride flat and featureless, thank you.*

"You didn't really want to go up that rock, did you," he says quietly, handing me another wipe when I need it for my knees.

Blinking to try to get rid of the moisture in my eyes, I avoid his eyes. "I guess not."

"Why didn't you walk it?"

"Nobody else did."

"Hm."

We're silent for a few moments while I finish cleaning the blood off my wounds. Even though he's quiet, I don't think he's judging me. He kind of acts like he's beating himself up.

"I'm sorry I didn't speak up," I say finally. "I guess the worst accidents probably happen when people aren't ready for something."

He nods slowly, wrapping gauze around my knee. "Yeah, but that's what we're supposed to be here for. Preparing you for the next thing we ask of you. We're not supposed to put you in a situation you're not ready for."

"It's not your fault," I say immediately. It isn't. Everyone else did fine with that feature. Only I couldn't wrap my head around it, much less my body. "I'm just slow."

"You're not slow," he snaps. He glances up at me and

smiles that small, sad smile again. "Maybe you'd benefit from more one-on-one instruction next time. I don't want you going into it feeling unsupported." He shrugs. "There's this book I like about different learning styles. Everyone's brain works differently and some people need to hear something several times. Other people need to read about it before they can repeat it. We need to figure out what works for you. We can do that."

"You think so?" I look over at my bike, laying on the ground nearby. Getting back on it is daunting, but Hunter has given me hope. Maybe something will eventually click and I'll actually enjoy this. As if it's a test I'm taking, maybe there's an answer.

"Definitely," he says confidently. The memory of hitting that bullseye, after his ax throwing lesson, makes me want to believe him.

Still, I... "Maybe we should start with something that won't leave me bleeding when I fail?"

"This is not a *fail*," Hunter says calmly, as he packs up the first aid supplies. "You fell down. That's part of the process. You took a step toward experience."

A step toward experience. I like the phrase, but my sore hands and knees don't appreciate it.

"I'm not going to let you avoid getting back on the bike," Hunter goes on. "We can definitely practice on something else to build up your confidence. I'll give you some one-on-one lessons if it will help."

"That would definitely help," I blurt. There I go again—brain and body disconnection. Or maybe it's a brain and heart disconnection, in this case. I want to spend more time with Hunter. The act of being around him makes me more confident. "I mean. You're a good teacher."

He smiles, and instead of standing up, he sits down on the ground beside me. "We can try axe throwing," he suggests. "It's nothing like riding a bike, but it's something you could get good at if you practice."

I'm not so sure about that. There are times when, no matter how much advice I hear about a topic, I still can't quite repeat the actions that would lead to success. I have this problem dating, too. My mom is always telling me that repeating something over and over while expecting a different outcome is the definition of insanity. She's usually referring to using Tinder.

"What if we start with something that doesn't involve sharp edges?" I suggest, timidly. "Like...skipping a rock!"

He laughs, putting a knee in the dirt beside me. "You want to learn how to skip a rock?"

"It's something I've never done before," I defend myself. "I tried the other day at the lake and my rock sank right away."

"OK," Hunter nods. "I can show you that. And we can paddle-board again. I guess the drawback of this adventure tour is we only give you shallow experiences. You don't have a chance to become an expert at anything." He pauses, like he's considering this.

The way his forehead wrinkles when he's thinking is so sweet. I watch a bead of sweat trace down his exposed chest and think about how he'd taste salty. Hunter is a sensuous experience. Being around him is like what I imagine the best camping trip would be: full of adventurous days and soothing nights. Like looking up at the stars in an endless night sky or standing perfectly balanced on the edge of a rock ledge.

I want to touch him. The way he touched me, so gently, winding the gauze around my knees and hands, made me wonder how he'd touch me without an injury as an excuse. Would he throw me around, using those muscles I can see in his arms and thighs? No. Hunter would be as gentle as he is when he's teaching me something. He would ask me questions and guide me to...well, to wherever we are going in this hypothetical fantasy.

And I wouldn't be scared, either. Not in the world I'm inventing in my head. Because Hunter would be there to give me one-on-one training and speak to me in the calm, confident voice he uses every time he teaches me something. I wonder if he uses that voice in bed, too?

"Maybe we should strip out some of the options so we can do activities more than once." Hunter is still musing out loud about the tour trips. It's clear he takes his job seriously.

It's hard not to chuckle.

"What?" he asks, already smiling back at me.

"I was just thinking about you kissing me and you're preoc-cupied with your work." *Oh shit! Yes, I said that.* Mind-body disconnect *again*.

Hunter is staring at me, unblinking. "You were thinking about kissing me? Right now? Why?"

This is such a bizarre question—it's so obvious!—it distracts me from my embarrassment. "Because you're...you. You're so kind and thoughtful. And you're sitting there with those huge calves and you look hot despite your pillow pants."

He tilts his head. "Despite them? I thought girls liked bike kits."

"I don't know what girls you are talking about, but you look very silly." And then I lean toward him. Not much, because I don't want to put my weight on my hand and he's too far away from me to reach without leverage. Still, I lean enough that he knows I wasn't joking about wanting to kiss him.

Because I'm trying new things and reaching for my dreams. I might fail a lot, but I keep going. *You have to have something to be proud of yourself for when you're as bad at as many things as I am.*

The only problem is, he's not leaning back.

seven

HUNTER

THE WORDS I heard Mollie's friend say are repeating over and over in my head: *You need some sexual adventure.*

I don't usually get involved with women only in town for an "adventure." I'm not a vending machine, and whatever I dispense would be a disappointment to the women looking for something more exciting and different compared to their "real" lives. I'm just me, and this town is pretty boring if you live here.

Scott can make a fling seem like an adventure. He's good at that.

But Mollie isn't trying to kiss Scott. She's leaning into *me.*

There are no books to guide me in this situation. None I've read, anyway. *How to kiss strangers without getting emotionally attached* would be helpful information right now.

Teasing her, or even being honest, could deflect the situation. *I don't know how to do this,* I could say. Mollie would be embarrassed and also understanding. And that would be that. I'd go on to teach her how to safely ride a mountain bike and she'd go home and forget about me.

Only there's something about the way Mollie has been so determined to keep trying. The way she acknowledges she's bad at these activities, like she straight-up acknowledged she was thinking about kissing me. I've never met someone so willing to fail over and over again.

I don't want her to fail now.

When we touch lips, I no longer feel the heat of the sun on my back or the dirt under my hands. Mollie makes a small sound that I also heard her make when she threw an axe the other day, a tiny grunt of release. This time, she hits the target. Our kiss is effortless, my head turning to the right while she turns to the left. Our tongues touching lightly. I'm getting hard and these bike shorts hide nothing.

It's been a while since I touched a woman intimately. Usually, I know her for a while first and I'd be more in my head when I finally kiss her. It would be more of an intellectual connection.

Holy shit, something different *is good.*

Reaching out, I let myself touch her arm, trailing my fingers down it. Her skin is soft. I wouldn't mind being wrapped up in it.

That second is all I get to imagine laying Mollie down on this rocky ground and getting lost in her when two cyclists not with our group blow past us, over the feature, and up the hill. We pull apart, watching them disappear.

"They make it look so easy," says Mollie, her face wistful.

I watch her face, the furrow between her eyebrows over her sunglasses, and I wish her eyes were visible. What did that kiss mean to her? Did she get the same zing of surprise that I did? The startling need to sink into *us* for a while?

Her gaze is following the other cyclists, not lingering on my lips. I swallow and force myself to move on. I debate telling her that on the full-suspension bike she's borrowing, she could have rolled up and over that feature easily without listening to any of the for-practice guidance Scott and I offered. If only she didn't hit the brakes.

Nah. If it's not easy for her, that's all that matters. Not whether it *should* be. "We'll get you there," I say simply, and study her face for signs she doesn't want to try again. I'm not a good enough teacher to beat resistance. But she looks at the little hill we're sitting next to as if it's one of Colorado's 14,000-foot mountains. Like it's meant to be climbed.

I'd sort of like her to look at me like that.

"Can you really teach me how to do that?" she asks, still not looking at me. "I'm...pretty bad at this."

"I can *absolutely* teach you how to do that," I reply. "You can be good at this. It takes some time. And practice."

She nods, like that settles it. Then she looks at me. "I know you only kissed me to encourage me," she says, matter-of-factly. "I appreciate it."

She carefully stands up, without bracing her hands on the ground, and brushes herself off. I stare up at her, letting my crotch know we're done here. It's slow to get the message.

"Mollie..."

Pausing, she looks back.

I *did* kiss her to be encouraging, at least a little. But I wouldn't have done it if I hadn't wanted to. I've never felt this way about someone on one of our tours. A little protective, and also...like I want to claim something. I wanted to get there first. Before Scott, or some other guy she might have turned to for her vacation "adventure." Was that enough? Was that all she wanted? Just a kiss?

"You'll get there," I mumble, falling back on my job. On being a guide who can work with anybody. Even a woman who turned my whole ethos upside down in one move.

* * *

When we rejoin the others, walking our bikes to get back to the trailhead, Mollie leaves my side with a polite smile to catch up with her friends.

"She OK?" Scott asks, pausing by my side to watch Mollie showing off her war wounds to Nora and Sophie.

Mollie seems to have bounced back from the fall—and the kiss—like it's something she does all the time. I don't want to assume, but maybe she does. "She's resilient," I say.

We close out the day's lesson with a few more brake exercises. I make sure Mollie gets back on the bike for a final lesson, yet avoid interacting with her much. She keeps smiling at me—only in a friendly way. Not like we shared something back there that's unusual. For me, at least.

After we herd everyone back to the center and put away their bikes, I'm walking back to my room when I hear Mollie with her two friends through the open window of the lobby. They're filling up their water bottles at the cooler.

"It looked like you had a moment," one of the other two women is saying. Her voice sing-songs on the word "moment" and I know instantly that they're talking about Mollie and me. I freeze, lurking outside the window frame where they can't see me. The amount of overhearing I'm doing lately is getting ridiculous—but I'm not about to walk away from Mollie's response. I know this is about me. Again.

"He's really nice," Mollie says. "And smart. He's so good at this stuff."

"Annnnnnd?" one of her friends cajoles. There's a pause.

"We kissed," Mollie admits.

"I knew it!"

"Way to go, Mollie. Vacation fling here you come." I can't tell which it is, but one of Mollie's friends sounds delighted.

"Here *you* come," the other one laughs. "I've seen you flirting with Scott."

"Hey, this isn't about me. How proud am I that you took my advice and actually went for it? This could be so good for you. When are you going to see him again?"

"Um…" Mollie sounds hesitant. And no wonder; she hadn't seemed that into our kiss. I look down at my feet. I'm standing in some Indian Paintbrush. I kneel and try to fluff up what I inadvertently trampled on. Maybe I'll look innocent if I'm caught, not like I'm eavesdropping.

"Mollie, *tell me* you did *not* leave it at a kiss."

"He said he'd help me practice some of the adventure stuff."

Both of Mollie's friends laugh. "I bet he'll help you *practice*."

"Did you get his number?"

"You need to go find him right now and set up your next meeting. We'll wait."

"But…"

"Have I steered you wrong yet? Go!"

Jumping out of my crouch, I start walking back the way I came, trying to put some distance between me and the window. As a result, I nearly run into Mollie coming out of the door of the adventure center.

"Oh, hi." We both stop and stare at each other awkwardly.

"I wondered," Mollie starts in a rush as I say, "Are you still interested…"

We both halt. Then we smile at each other.

"Could we do those private lessons you mentioned? I know it's a lot to ask," Mollie says. "I thought I'd improve a lot faster if you showed me some things one-on-one."

"Of course. I wouldn't have offered if I didn't mean it." I pull out my phone. "Why don't you give me your number so we can set it up."

After she does, I linger, shifting my weight back and forth on my feet as I wonder how to bring up the kiss. Or her friends concluding I'm her "vacation fling." Or my uncharacteristic interest in being that. I wonder if they're still listening, right on the other side of the door.

"Well, I better…" she begins as I say, "About the…"

We both stop and, again, stare at each other. She smiles and I smile back.

"I could use the practice," she says. "At everything you've showed me so far."

"Even the…" I blink.

"Yeah. Especially that."

Well, I'm pretty sure I know what we're talking about here, but I'm not used to playing games in my conversations. "I thought you did pretty well at the kissing part," I say.

She grins. "Then maybe I can show you something in return." She winces. "Not that you don't know what you're doing. You're very…talented."

"Thanks. I read a lot of books." Because now I can't help it, I laugh. I hope her friends aren't eavesdropping right now, discovering how very *not* smooth I am. She laughs with me.

"OK, well…" she gestures vaguely over her shoulder. I nod.

"I'll text you later," I say. "Maybe tomorrow morning? If you're OK getting up early."

"I'm totally OK with that."

"Great."

"I'll see you, Hunter." I think it's the first time she's said my name to my face. I nod.

"See you, Mollie."

Are all hook-ups this awkward to arrange? I wouldn't know. This is my first one.

* * *

We meet at a small pond not far outside of town. "Nora and Sophie weren't even up yet when I left the hotel this morning,"

Mollie tells me conspiratorially. She seems delighted that I brought her coffee and her favorite muffin—the lemon curd—from Dorothy's and not sorry to see the sun start to rise over the mountains surrounding us.

The early morning sun illuminates her in a way I've never seen before. She's golden and happy and I'm not sorry I got up and left on one of the few mornings I could have slept in a little, either.

It's technically a day off for Mollie's group on the tour. We planted one early in the week so that we didn't burn people out on activities too soon. Scott's taking another group out hiking today, while I need to plan the logistics of the next few outings and run inventory.

And hang out with Mollie. I'm already thinking of inviting her to the lake later.

"So, first, we find a rock. You want a kind of flat one." I start looking around on the ground.

Mollie stands nearby, sipping her coffee and watching me. "You're so earnest."

"Does it bother you?" I've heard that before, usually toward the end of a relationship when they got tired of me.

"No, I'm worried I won't be good at this and disappoint you."

"The only thing you have to do is try. The results don't matter to me. If you try and you enjoy the process a little bit, that's all I want."

She smiles. "Really? Are you sure you don't want me to become a stone-throwing savant at least a *little* bit? You know, because you're such a good teacher."

Looking around my feet at the rocks, I consider it. "I know I'm kind of serious about this stuff."

"Kind of."

"It's because I want people to enjoy it as much as I do. That's why I like teaching, not because I want to prove I can make people better at something. People who say anyone can be taught, or whatever, are inflating the ego of the teacher. Learning is a partnership. And you and I are still getting to know each other."

Then spotting a perfect rock, I pick it up.

Mollie is still eying me when I approach her with it. "Do you journal? You talk like someone who's figured out their thoughts."

Extending the rock to her, I nod. "Cheaper than therapy."

She takes and examines it.

"When you release the rock, you want to let it kind of roll off your fingers. Like this." I demonstrate with my hand without throwing the stone. "Actually," I add, and pick up another rock. "Why don't you try it once first and let me see what we're working with."

She makes a face, but gamely hands me her paper coffee cup and takes the rock.

I don't use the phrase "throws like a girl"—it really means "throws like someone who's never been taught how"—so I don't apply it to Mollie's attempt. She doesn't turn her body and she throws overhand, so the rock sinks in the water like...well, like a stone.

She makes a face when she turns back to me. "Not good, huh?"

"Did you never play sports growing up?"

She shakes her head. "Shows, huh?"

"This is another simple muscle memory thing. Once we train your muscles on what they're supposed to do, you'll have a better chance of accurately throwing whatever you want. Axes, balls, rocks."

Her eyes brighten, my favorite thing in the world. I love when people get excited about potential learning, and that goes double for Mollie. In the golden light that's going to make us put on our sunglasses soon, her eyes are brilliant.

"Really?" she asks.

"Really. It does take some practice. And starting gradually, so you don't hurt yourself and set your progress back." We start there, with me showing her how to throw with her body instead of only her shoulder.

I use my hands, with permission, to show her how to twist her whole body and step forward with her non-dominant leg and then follow through with the throw. "If you do it right, you can put all the energy from your entire body, from your feet up to your hand, into your throw. That's called kinetic linking."

She confesses, "I don't really get it." But she keeps practicing, showing me how she'd turn into it without throwing yet.

"Then let it go when it's going the direction you want," I tell her, once I think she's got the turning motion down.

She gives me a face like I've overwhelmed her with directions.

"Do you want to pause and eat your muffin?" I suggest.

"Yes!" She almost bounces when we walk over to a bench to sit down. She'd talked about how good this muffin was when we went on the bike outing. She made it sound like the best thing she'd ever eaten, so I had to get one for myself.

And it's good, I guess, like everything from Dorothy's is good. She gets some of her pastries from the Arnauds and bakes the rest in-house so they're all handmade.

The best part about it is watching Mollie enjoy hers. "People always talk about how good the food is in cities," she sighs, licking crumbs off her fingers. "But there's something about food in a small town. At least *this* small town. Do you think it's the air?"

"It's made with love," I offer, fully aware it's cheesy. "And not by a machine."

"That must be it!"

I let her enjoy her crumbs in the quiet. There are few people walking around yet this morning and the air is chilly and still. It's nice hanging out with her. Eventually, I ask, "Ready to give it a try?"

Nervously, she nods. She bites her lip.

"You might not get it the first time, but you can keep trying," I reassure her. "We have plenty of time."

She does not, in fact, get it the first time. I keep coaching her, showing her on a few stones of my own. I can tell she's getting discouraged after the fourth or fifth attempt. She's releasing her stones too early or too late, not turning her body enough, or forgetting to step forward on one leg. Her brain hasn't quite latched onto the concept of channeling energy.

"Try using your left hand to point at where you want the rock to go," I suggest. "And then throw the rock when you're aiming that direction."

She tries it, putting all my tips together, and the rock skips once before it sinks. She shrieks. "I did it!"

Her enthusiasm is so genuine, my heart skips a beat. She's jumping in the air and I hold out my arms because it seems like the thing to do. And then I'm holding her.

We meet each others' eyes, and the energy buzzes in my feet, traveling up my legs and torso and into the arms wrapped around her. Neither of us step away and so I release the energy by lowering my head to hers.

When we kiss this time, it doesn't feel like a consolation prize. It feels like joy.

eight

MOLLIE

I NEVER SHOULD HAVE LET Nora and Sophie believe I was off to hook up with Hunter.

Sophie made me borrow her underwire bikini top that makes my boobs look like a cliff. "It worked for me," she told me with a wink.

Nora painted my toenails to match the color of the bathing suit. "It's a subconscious clue the carpet and drapes match, you know what I mean?" she joked.

Admitting the only reason I'm meeting Hunter this afternoon is to get in extra practice would have been worse. Nora and Sophie are effortlessly good at everything. They won't understand that I need to try, and try, and try again in order to get it. They'd tease me for not wanting to spend my time under a hot instructor learning *other* things about my body.

And it's not that I'm not interested in Hunter like that. This morning was a revelation. Spending time with Hunter felt like a date wrapped up in a lesson or vice versa. But I've felt so incompetent so far this vacation that expanding my capacity to have adventures sounds even more satisfying than sex at the moment.

When I get to the adventure center, I realize I'll be under Hunter, after all, because he's only got one stand-up paddleboard out and he says I can sit in the front while he paddles standing over me. "This will give you a chance to get a better feel for the board," he says. I'll definitely get a *feel* for something if I'm holding onto his legs with a death grip.

He sees from my face that I'm uncertain. "You need a distraction," he announces. "How about..." he hesitates, like he has to work up the nerve to suggest this. "A kiss for every time you try something hard."

"How do we define 'hard'?" I volley back, not because I don't want to say "yes" but because I want more kisses. Then I realize what I said.

"Hard is in the eye of the beholder," he says. He grins back at me. "So it's however you define it."

"And I just have to try? Not succeed?" That's basically what he promised me that morning, and it's too good to be true.

"That's right."

"This seems like a pretty good deal for me," I say suspiciously.

"Hmm, I've seen you try things over and over again. Pretty sure I'm getting the better deal."

And so off we go on the single paddleboard, me awkwardly sitting with my legs criss-crossed in front of Hunter, who stands up with the paddle. I keep checking my crotch to make sure I'm not exposing more than I intend in my bikini bottoms. When I try to rearrange my limbs, the entire board sways. My toes get splashed with cold lake water.

"It's OK. This board is more stable than you think," Hunter says. He starts wiggling the board by moving his legs, tilting it back and forth between his weight, and I shriek. "See? It's hard to tip!"

I grab his ankle and he stops. If I tilt my head back, I'm looking at his shorts. So I stare straight ahead while I answer. "It's like we're standing on air in the middle of a giant lake." I'm absolutely positive that we're going to end up in the lake at some point on this adventure. It's a matter of when.

He laughs. "People know we're out here. I left word at the center. If that makes you feel better."

"The lifejacket makes me feel better," I sigh, putting my hands on both sides of the jacket that keeps pulling up around my ears.

"See? Falling in isn't the worst thing in the world."

"I'd rather decide when I want to go in." Then I grimace. I sound so whiny, even to my own ears. At least I'm not sitting in a windowless office all day. This could be *fun* if I let it. "OK," I say, partly to myself. "Let me try."

I can hear him grinning when he replies, "You got it!"

Switching places is a delicate dance. He gets down on his knees, the paddleboard swaying, and I get up on mine. I turn so I'm partly facing him. Now we're face to face and I'm thinking about my promised reward.

He's not grinning anymore. His face is serious, his blue eyes searching. He's waiting on me to move.

Well, he didn't specify *what* I'd be trying that was hard—and this, right now, seems to qualify. I'm staring back at a man I'd like to kiss and I'm frozen. My knees are objecting to the hard board. My hands are wet from a pool of water beneath us. Our positions feel precarious. Yet he told me I could kiss him and for some reason, I haven't. *Silly Mollie. You can do this.* And I do. I lean forward and kiss Hunter.

His lips are warm compared to the water evaporating off my skin. He's a little salty and he tastes like the sun. I pull back when he puts his hand on my arm. "I haven't tried the thing yet."

He smiles again, tucking his chin like he's abashed. "Very disciplined."

He helps me maneuver so I'm behind him, shifting knee-over-knee until I'm on the back of the board. He gives me the same spiel he'd given me the other day, all of it familiar but already nearly forgotten when I try to repeat it. "You want to be slightly behind the middle of the board, and when you stand up, you want to spread your feet so you have a good center of gravity. Don't lock your knees. And give yourself some time to adjust because the blood is going to rush to your head after kneeling."

He's absolutely right. When I stand up, I almost sit back down again immediately, because I get dizzy. Hunter holds me around the waist from his kneeling position and grounds me.

"Holy shit, I feel high," I say, once I open my eyes again. There's nothing but water around us, the shore far away. Will I ever get used to this? Hunter won't always be there to save me from falling, or reassure me I won't. Right now, I genuinely don't know what I'd do without him.

"Look at me," Hunter says, and I do. His eyes are steady. "One paddle at a time is how we get to where we're going."

"OK." I take a deep breath and hold the paddle the way he showed me before we left the dock, trying to push-pull with my two hands as I tow it toward me in the water. After a few strokes, we start to move. We're turning, but we're moving! I decide turning toward shore was my goal and go with it, skimming us across the water. I'm not as fast as Hunter, my strokes not half as powerful. I'm still doing it. The board is moving under my own power. And I'm standing! Unlike the other day, I'm doing this the way the name implies I should.

"Don't get too close to shore on this side," Hunter says quietly. He's facing forward now, and I've been partially bracing my—bent!—knees against his back. "There are those over-hanging trees. It's not that big of a deal on this lake, but on a river you could get caught in a strainer."

I stop paddling. We keep drifting toward shore, though. "I don't know what that means, but it sounds bad."

"It's undergrowth that we could get trapped in. If we get pulled under, it's hard to get out of underwater roots and we could drown."

Immediately, I start paddling on the other side, veering away from the shore again. I am *not* going to drown today.

"My feet are starting to hurt," I say after we're safely back into the middle of the lake. "Is that normal?"

"They're not used to balancing on the board. Very normal. Do you want to sit down again?"

We perform the same maneuver again, carefully trying to switch places without touching the water. Well, I'm trying not to touch the water. Hunter splashes me with the smallest handful before he slides to the side and pauses, face-to-face with me again.

"I'm afraid to close my eyes," I confess. "Are we going to fall off of this thing?"

"Well, one way to solve this problem would be to lower your center of gravity," Hunter says. It takes me a moment to follow his logic, because he says it in his "coach" voice, the one he uses to keep me from panicking.

"You mean lay down?"

He shrugs, tucking his chin again. "If you want to."

"It sounds hard. I'll do it." After all, hard gets rewarded around here.

Slowly, I manage to get my legs out from under me. I try to lay down but the lifejacket gets in the way, so I take it off and tuck it under one of the bungee cords wrapped around the paddleboard. Then I lay prone on the board on my back. Hunter stands to get out of my way, straddling me from above. He grins down at me. "Not so hard, was it?"

I pause a moment before I answer, working up the courage. "Well, not yet," I say, and raise my sunglasses for a moment to wink at him. Then I put them back on, because my eyes start watering from the sun.

He laughs. "I wouldn't depend on that," he says, and his voice sounds a little strained. I wonder how I look, laying beneath him like this, my big boobs filling out this bikini top nicely. I'm often self-conscious of my curvy body, but out here in front of no one except Hunter, I'm not worried.

Hunter lowers himself onto his knees, still straddling me, then down onto his hands. He attaches the paddle to the board with the velcro straps and takes off his lifejacket, too.

Then he pauses and looks at me. "You look nervous. Is this *too* hard?"

"I don't know, is it?" I grin. I can't stop teasing him. He takes it so well and it's fun. "I'm nervous about the board, not you."

"It won't flip, I promise. This board really can't do that." He hovers over me, and his thighs must be rock-solid because he barely moves and neither does the board.

Using the fingers of the hand not holding onto the side of the board with white knuckles, I gesture for him to get closer. He's heavy on top of me, and the board does rock a little when he lies down. There's zero room for us to lay side-by-side, so he holds himself up on his elbows over me. He can't hide a thing from me now, with his crotch next to mine. I laugh a little to cover my shiver at the position.

"What?"

"This is not what I expected from your one-on-one lessons. I like it!" I add quickly, because he moves to get off me.

"I've never done anything quite like this," he admits. "It's... not very professional."

"You don't usually train the tourists this way?"

"Never." He looks serious when he says that.

And I like hearing it—that I'm the first tourist he's laid on top of out here. It's a little hard to believe. Hunter is different than Sophie and Nora think. He's quiet and thoughtful. But he's also got a body like Chris Hemsworth and the blue eyes of Paul Hollywood. "What about a local?"

He laughs lightly. "I have never gotten horizontal on a paddleboard with another woman, ever. This is a first."

"Then I'm a lucky girl." I'm babbling and he knows it. I swallow my nervousness and say, "Now what are we going to do in this position, Mr. Tour Guide?"

"Well..." He adjusts and his body skims over mine, raising goosebumps on my bare skin. Then he says in his coaching voice, "If you turn your head a little and close your eyes, that means I can kiss you."

I angle my head to the left.

Close my eyes.

And wait, tuned into the sounds of the birds and the rippling water around us, and the places where his bare skin meets mine. He's warm, even though he's blocking the sun, so warm even the puddles of water beneath me are comfortable.

Then he kisses me. His lips are soft—kind, like him—and warm, gliding over my mouth gently until I open my own lips and let him in. It's beginning to be familiar, this meeting of our skin. Yet it's still so consuming I tune out the rocking of the board beneath us, the sound of the water rippling.

We spend several minutes or more like that, exploring each other with only the fish as witnesses. Then I start to notice something moving between my inner thighs. I startle, like a dummy, because my first thought is something has made its way onto the board with us. Then I realize it's Hunter, growing hard against my leg.

"Oh my, I appear to have caught a big fish," I say, and he laughs, resting his forehead against mine, because we're good at being silly together. I'd never say that in front of my friends. Or any of my recent lovers. I can't imagine being that comfortable with any of them, especially this soon after meeting.

"Don't worry, it'll go away if you ignore it," he says. "I like doing what we're doing."

"Me too."

Then the breeze sweeps between us and I shiver.

"Are you cold?" he immediately starts gathering himself to get up, getting one knee under him on my right side.

"No, I'm OK!" I insist quickly, shifting to grab him greedily back to me. The board rocks to the right when I do and I freeze, clutching him to me chest-to-chest.

"These boards really are stable, I promise," he tells me, his breath whispering over my lips because he's so close to me. The board rocks back to center and stops, barely moving on the water.

"I don't know what I'm afraid of. If we fell in, we'd get right back on the board, right?" I crane my neck, not letting go of Hunter, and check to see whether we're drifting closer to shore. We're still in the middle of the lake.

So we make out some more, lazily, drifting along on the board in the sun. I start to relax, forgetting I'm on a board made of air in the middle of a body of water.

That's when a whistle blasts through the air and makes Hunter leap off me, jumping to his feet. He immediately tips over, tries to balance on one foot to avoid stepping on me, and then falls in. "Fuck you, Scott!" he yells as he goes. Stupidly, I try to grab him, and slide off the board after him in slow-motion, grabbing at the sides as I go. The water is a shock, cold against my sun-heated skin.

I never quite submerge because I manage to grab the board

to keep my head above water. It's icy cold. I'm sure this water comes straight from the mountains. Scott is on a paddle board to our left, laughing his ass off and doubled over clutching his stomach. I blink at him. To go from Hunter warm and on top of me to this freezing lake is disorienting.

Hunter resurfaces and grabs onto the board, which has already regained equilibrium. He's right, this thing really is stable. "Are you OK?" he asks me. I nod, shivering.

"You guys could've seen me coming for the last 20 minutes but I guess you were *busy*." Scott is remorseless.

Hunter looks over at me, and before I can stop myself, I'm brushing the wet hair out of his eyes. My hand trembles when I touch him. "I'm sorry, my friend here is an asshole," he says. He raises his voice on the last word, looking over his shoulder at Scott, who is still grinning.

"You know, paddleboarding is normally done standing up. I thought you guys had some kind of medical emergency out here. I was worried," Scott continues, smirking through his deadpan words. "So I came to check."

"Sure you did," Hunter replies.

"Plus, you're not wearing life vests." He clicks his tongue disapprovingly. Hunter actually looks a little abashed, despite his irritation with the other guide. I know we weren't actually being unsafe, but Hunter is such a professional about everything that I feel bad.

"In all seriousness, did you notice the wind is coming up?" Scott points at the sky to the west. There are dark clouds moving in rapidly, I realize.

"Oh," I say.

"I came to warn you," Scott says. He brushes off his shoulder. "Good thing I was here, huh?"

Hunter rolls his eyes. "I guess we better paddle in," he tells me. "You first," he adds to me, and I take a deep breath and use my arms for leverage to lift myself back aboard. I lean to the other side of the board when he does the same.

"Bet you learned a lot from today's lesson, huh?" Scott asks me, using his paddle to turn his board back toward shore. "Pop quiz later! Be ready!"

"Paddle us back in," Hunter says, pulling the paddle out of the velcro straps on the side of the board and offering it to me.

"Me?" I squeak. "Don't we need to hurry?" The wind *is* starting to pick up and I'm afraid to stand.

Kneeling in front of me, holding out the paddle, Hunter smiles easily. "We have plenty of time. You've got this. It'll warm you up. You can kneel while you paddle if it makes you more comfortable."

He read my mind. I take the paddle. "OK, I'll give it a shot."

Leaning in, he says softly, "Want your reward now or later, when we have more privacy?"

I'm pleased to hear our deal still stands later. I bite my lip. "Later," I say.

"Later," he agrees, like it's a promise. And with Hunter, I believe it is.

nine

HUNTER

ONCE THE SUN GOES DOWN, the guys who rent rooms in Tom's house tend to gather in the living room. Scott is playing Madden with Tyler, who doesn't live here but works for Tom part-time and is the acknowledged expert at Madden—given he used to play professional football. Tom is doing a cross-word puzzle in the local newspaper. I'm reading my book, the latest from Ta-Nehisi Coates.

"Did you hear Hunter has a girlfriend?" Scott nudges Tyler, as they sit side-by-side with their controllers.

Tom looks up.

"I don't have a girlfriend," I protest. I get stuck after that, because I don't know what Mollie is and insisting it's "just a summer fling" would be disingenuous. Plus, no one would believe me. "You're one to talk!" I fire back instead.

Tyler smirks and nudges Scott back. "He's got you there. Who's your flavor of the season?"

"Hey, I've never been caught making out in the middle of the lake."

"'Never been caught' are the operative words there," Tom grumbles. As a boss and landlord, Tom is pretty compartmentalized. He watches closely on matters of safety and lets us live our lives otherwise—which clearly includes Scott's frequent dips into the pool of paying customers.

Tyler snorts. "What, on one of those tiny boards?" A huge man, most of our "gizmos" are toys to Tyler. He helps out sometimes when we get a large axe-throwing party and can handle a whitewater raft better than anyone, but he refuses to get on a horse, a paddleboard, or a bicycle for fear he'd "snap it like a twig."

"He fell in," Scott teases.

"That was *your* fault!" I protest. "And she fell in, too."

"Hey, don't go making out on a paddleboard if you can't handle getting wet." He twists his lips a little over the words "getting wet," and Tyler and Tom both smirk.

I kick Scott in the back—only a tap, yet enough to let him know I don't like this. He shouldn't talk about Mollie that way.

Scott drops his controller and turns around. "You're the one getting in too deep, man."

"I'm fine," I say, putting a bookmark in my book and getting ready to stand.

"Nah, you're too serious for this," Scott insists. He looks to Tyler and Tom for support. "Make sure you have the conversation."

"What conversation?" I shouldn't ask. But I do.

Scott groans, rolling his entire head back. "'What conversation', he says. Poor sweet summer child. The conversation about what this is and when it ends!"

"I don't know," Tyler says, as he crushes Scott on Madden while his back is turned. "Sometimes you don't know what it is and you get to explore it together." Tyler's been in an on-and-off-again relationship with the same woman for as long as we've known him. That's different. She's a local. They're also great together and everyone knows it, so we're all waiting for them to catch up.

"That's different," Scott says. "Mollie's not a local. She's going to leave at the end of the week. Then what, they're going to explore long-distance?"

Everyone in the room makes a face as we all recognize a potential sore spot. Tom was "seeing" someone long-distance when I first moved in. He never talks about her anymore and she never visited, so I assume that went in opposite directions the way very separate lives tend to do.

"It's temporary," I say. "I know that." Even I hear the way my voice sounds uncertain. Tom's gaze on me is steady. Concerned. *Shit.*

"Hey!" Scott turns back around and grabs his controller and I use the distraction to get up and leave the living room with my book.

Tom follows me into the kitchen.

"Scott's rough around the edges, but he means well."

"I know," I reply. I'm surprised Tom is bothering to follow up on this conversation. Much like Scott, Tom tends to be rough around the edges. He cares about us, I'm sure, and he'd rather stay out of our lives. I've heard him say "live and let live" more than once in my time staying and working here—once referring to Scott's heat-addled decision to sleep naked on the back porch. "You don't need to worry. I'm only giving her some private lessons. And having a little fun." I add the last part out of a personal obligation to be honest. It's the most true I can be without melting into a puddle of uncertainty. Hanging out with Mollie, if nothing else, *is* fun.

It's also more than that.

He nods. He gets a beer out of the fridge and, thankfully,

turns to leave. Then he pauses at the doorway. "Make sure you stop when it stops being fun, Hunter. Emotional pain is a warning just like your body hurting." He coughs, like he's embarrassed he said something so profound. "Wish I'd learned that at your age, that's all."

Then he leaves me alone to contemplate what I've gotten myself into.

* * *

I catch Mollie, Sophie, and Nora leaving Dorothy's coffee shop the next morning when I go to grab the usual coffee box we offer the tour guests. They all have cups in their hands that I bet are something more fancy than drip.

They don't see me coming because they've turned the other way down the street. The morning air has a nip to it and they're all wearing jackets. Mollie is even wearing a cute cap, her short hair poking out from beneath it in tufts.

Pausing at the coffee shop door as a few other people are coming out, I'm about to call out a greeting when Nora's words float back to me—making me an unwilling eavesdropper, yet again.

"You have to sleep with him," she's saying. "If you want a happy hour story that will last you a few years, at least."

"One you can go back to when you're old and gray," Sophie laughs. "The adventure guide who *taught* you memorable lessons that one hot summer."

"Or cold summer," Nora adds, and they keep walking so I can't hear anything else. I'm standing frozen on the sidewalk, and out of the corner of my eye I catch a movement that turns out to be Dorothy waving at me to come into her shop.

Pain. Is this the warning sign Tom told me to watch for? My

reaction to Mollie's friends is mild—*of course they're going to joke about us; didn't my own friends?*—but it's uncomfortable. I'm not sure how many warnings I get before it's too late, yet I'm not nearly ready to back away. Watching Mollie walk down the street away from me, I want to give her my scarf and tuck her close to keep her warm.

It's fine. We're having a little fun. So long as I keep it at the kissing level, it isn't going to hurt too much when she leaves.

I walk into the coffee shop and wave at Tyler, having breakfast with his girl Zoe. Dorothy is in a tizzy over gossip that Mark Wadson, the newspaper's editor, plans to retire. "Hasn't he said that every year for the last..." I try to remember. "Forever?"

"Rumor has it," she says in an undertone the entire coffee shop can hear, "he might be doing it for a woman." She raises her eyebrows at me, then pauses, like I might be able to identify the woman in question. I have no idea. I mostly stay out of town gossip, and try not to be a source or a subject.

"Unless she frequents the bookstore, I have no idea, Dorothy." I smile though, and then ask if my order is ready.

Carrying the coffee back to the adventure center, I get morose. Am I just going to keep reading about life for the rest of mine? That's what Scott and Tom expect. But I want to live, too. So what if that comes with a little pain? So do most of my hobbies. Right now, I have a jagged wound down one knee from mountain biking.

Because the truth is, I don't want to stay at the kissing level with Mollie. Maybe I need to do a little research about ethical flings. *How to Win Sex and Influence Strangers*? No, that's Scott's bible. I need something more like *The Subtle Art of Not Giving Your Heart.*

Hell, I've always wanted to write a book. Maybe this is my chance.

* * *

On our hike that day, I give Mollie and her friends a wide berth. It's not that I don't want to hang out with Mollie, it's that her friends are a lot. Scott doesn't mind; he picks up the slack and flirts with Nora all morning.

I can't help watching as Mollie listens closely—and follows—the lesson on staying on the trail. And then the basic lesson on orienteering. It's her turn to try to read the map after we break for lunch, and I watch her study the contour lines. She gets their meaning completely wrong, underestimating the elevation gain we're about to walk up—which gets some grumbles from the rest of the group—then she tries again and I see the moment the lesson clicks for her. That's my favorite moment in any class, and Mollie makes it even more special. I want to reward her for trying so badly my mouth purses, but I don't want to provide more fodder for her friends to joke about.

"This backpack is killing my neck," Nora tells Scott. I'm about to check whether it's properly fitted; Scott is quicker on the uptake.

"I'll give you a shoulder massage when we get back."

"Oh yeah? You good at that?"

"I don't have these strong hands for nothing." Scott flexes said hands as they walk, and I roll my eyes. He catches it out of the corner of his eye.

"Of course, I don't have a license, like Hunter, here."

Glaring at Scott, I see Nora nudge Mollie.

"You have a massage license?" Mollie asks.

Keeping my eyes on the rest of the group hiking in front of us, I shrug. Still the same number we left with and everyone is staying on the trail. "It's something I picked up. It comes in handy in my line of work sometimes."

"Now I'm picturing you and the guys back at the adventure center giving each other massages at the end of a long day," Nora says. "It's not a bad picture."

"Shirtless, obviously," Sophie adds.

"Obviously," Nora agrees.

"We unfortunately can't provide that service to everyone in the group," I say stiffly, wishing I'd avoided this conversation.

"And we don't expect it from you," Mollie says hastily, clearly trying to save me.

"*We* don't expect special treatment," Nora says, and she and Scott share a grin. "Although maybe *Mollie* can expect some... *special* treatment from you, Hunter."

Mollie is bright red. She's still walking, but her hands look frozen in place at her sides. Her body language screams that she doesn't know what to do.

"I don't know that Mollie wants special treatment," I say slowly.

Nora opens her mouth, and Sophie smacks her arm. Scott is watching this exchange like he wishes he had popcorn.

And then I decide to speak up. Because, if there was a manual for this situation, it would remind me that time is short and I only have a few days with this woman. I might as well enjoy them. "If she does, I'd be happy to provide a massage back at the lodge, though. Or my place." I tack on the last bit because if I'm going to be bold, I might as well go all the way. I've blamed Tom for not wanting to step out farther onto this limb, yet Tom won't care, not really. He might hold me to a higher standard than he does Scott, but he won't hold it against me if I have a little fun. Right?

Mollie's startled eyes meet mine. It's possible I've taken this too far, and still, despite all our friends watching and drawing their own conclusions, I don't care. I want Mollie to know I'm here for *her*.

Then she smiles at me, and it's like we're alone in this forest together. "I'd like that," she says. "It's a date."

Then it's settled. Because I know one date won't be enough for me with this woman, and more than that can only mean one thing. We're having a summer fling.

ten

MOLLIE

I'M NOT sure what to expect from a shared house where a bunch of outdoorsy guys live. Perhaps muddy shoes everywhere, mountains of beer cans, and athletic gear stored in the pantry.

But the house Hunter takes me to, which is near the adventure center, looks like my parents' house and is maintained about as well. There's a nice wrap-around porch—swept clean—and while the front room *is* full of gear and shoes, everything is lined up in rows and tidy piles. The dining room table is full of maps and guidebooks—words like "rock climbing" and *Utah's 50 Best Hikes* and *Colorado's Fourteeners* jump out at me but I don't poke around.

When Hunter directs me to his room, down a hallway of closed doors, I stop in the doorway and close my mouth. His room is filled with books. There are two full bookshelves against one wall by a desk, and there are also stacks everywhere. There's a stack on his nightstand and another on the floor by the bed. There's a stack on the windowsill, propping open the window, and another by the door-jam as we walk in.

Most of the stacks have bookmarks poking out of some of the books.

"How many of these are you reading at the same time?" I ask, turning in a circle once I manage to cross the threshold of the room. I'm surrounded by more reading material than I've seen anywhere outside a library. "And how many do you read every year?"

Hunter stands barely inside the door with his hands tucked in the pockets of his jeans. "I'm kind of a grazer. I read a chapter here and there when it's relevant to my interests at the time. I don't always follow through on reading the whole book. Often, I come back to things."

"Are there more in your closet?"

He laughs a little. "Maybe a few."

Moving slowly to give him the chance to protest, I walk over to the closed closet door and open it. Even under a pair of cleated bike shoes, there are a few more books. *No skeletons in this closet, merely a well-rounded man.*

I wasn't expecting my emotional reaction to that, like a punch to the throat. Getting to know Hunter is hard, because everything he reveals about himself makes me want to know more. I want to hug all this information, along with the man himself, close to my chest and squeeze. I can't be the only woman to have seen this closet—*can I?*—and I wonder if we've all reacted this way. And all lost him in the end, this man who is so much more than we expected.

Swallowing back all the feels, I face him. "I like it," I say.

His mouth tugs up into a grin. "Sorry there's not really anywhere to sit." He pulls out the desk chair and moves the stack of books off it, offering it to me.

I look between the offered chair and the bed. With a bite of my lower lip, I choose the bed. I'm not here for a relationship. There's no reason to pretend otherwise. This is a temporary arrangement between Hunter and me. I need to keep my eye on what I want to get out of it, as Nora said to me before slapping my butt and sending me off to "have fun" after the hike.

Nora and Sophie mean well. But they're much more certain about everything than I am. When I'm around them, I often adopt what *they* want because it's so much easier than figuring out what I do.

I want to sleep with Hunter. I do.

But I'm still second-guessing my choice of seat. Because what if my own closet is filled with feelings and they all come pouring out, turning this into an impossible situation for both of us?

Hunter picks up one of his books and sits down on the bed beside me. "This is going to sound like a line, but I can't help it. I haven't had a woman in my room in a long time, so I've gotta ask. A couple of months ago I tried to find a book to read that portrayed the female perspective, and it involved a lot of trial and error and I eventually read this. Do you think it fits the bill?" He holds the book up, allowing me to read it's title: *We Should All Be Feminists*.

"I haven't read that," I admit, ignoring the tingle in my lady parts. "Are you sure this *isn't* a line? Did you take that book to the bars and wait for women to approach you? Because I feel like it would work."

"No." He grimaces. "Although, Scott suggested it. So I thought about it. I never did. I was too interested in actually reading the book. I didn't want to be interrupted."

"That's fair." My heart squeezes from how adorable this man is.

"In complete transparency, after I finished the book, Scott tried it out and he said it worked really well." Hunter puts the book back on the stack on the floor by his bed.

"Could you *hear* it working really well?" I gesture at the walls of his bedroom. "How thin are these?"

"Yeah, you called that. They're pretty bad," he admits. "Usually nobody's here during the day." He winces and looks at his hands as he adds, "If you're worried about that. Not that you have any reason to be."

His darkening cheeks make me want to be the bold one. It's not Nora and Sophie urging me on in this moment, it's the fact that foreplay with Hunter involves a literary discussion.

"Hunter," I say. "Let's be real here. We want to have sex. And I'd rather no one be listening to us."

He meets my eyes. His blue ones are surprised only briefly, then turn thoughtful. "I guess I shouldn't be surprised you are so straightforward about this."

"No? Most people would be." The truth is, Hunter's one of the only people I would *be* so straightforward with. It's easy to be brave around him. *Sweet and daring.* The gentle way he coaxes her out of me makes it easy for me to be the woman he seems to see.

"No," he says. "You're spicy, remember? And daring. You're one of the only people I know who doesn't, you know, grandstand or coat everything with a layer of bullshit. Even my friends —even though I love them—they can't have a heart-to-heart conversation without pretending they're joking around."

"I just coat everything with a layer of failure instead." I laugh, then wince. "Sorry. That was bullshit, like you said. I know I fail a lot but not *every* time."

"So long as you keep trying, anyway." He grins. "Success is the result of as many fails as you're willing to give. Remember when I taught you about sessioning, on the bike? That's the same thing. You repeat it over and over, breaking it down into achievable parts, until you succeed at the whole thing."

"That seems like a life approach." I mean it. I'm not agreeing only because Hunter's nearness is getting to me. And despite being brave, despite my personal determination to live without bullshit, I'm still struggling to reach between us and touch him. I need him to make the first move.

"What if we approach this like that?" he murmurs, twisting toward me. "When I look at you, there are a lot of parts I want to...well—a *lot* of things I want to do. And touch. So maybe we break it down and take it slow?"

Slow is not what I'm used to, and I should have expected it from this man. His care—the way he waits for me to answer before he reaches out—makes me bold again. "And maybe you could start by touching me here?" I rest my hand on my thigh.

"I like a map." He puts his hand there.

"More like a guidebook, I think," I reply, laying down on my back with my legs still dangling off the bed. "I didn't give you the contour lines."

He grins, leaning over me propped on his elbow, one hand still tracing the seam of my jeans. "Look how well you listen."

We both know I wasn't actually any good at the contour lines. This is something I can do, though. I can present my own body to explore. There's nothing else I want more in this moment. "Anything else you want to teach me?"

He pauses, looking down at what his hand is doing. "I'd like to learn the contour lines of your body. Is that OK?"

Mutely, I nod, because I'm holding my breath for what I think is going to happen next. And then, Hunter puts both hands on me. He slides them up my body, over the swell of my breasts, where he pauses to feel my nipples perk against his palms.

Oh my god, so this is what elevation gain is really like. The rush goes straight to my head. Every part of me is attuned to his hands, to the next turn they might take as they explore.

He runs his hands over all of me, from my collarbones to my toes after he takes off my shoes. From the look of concentration on his face, I think he really is learning my dimensions. It feels as if he's not just touching me, but every inch of me onto the map he's creating with his hands.

His hands study me. And I study back, sensitized to every pressure change, to the way his hands caress around my breasts and then firmly grasp my hips. The way he maps me tells me he knows what to do with my body, from my flesh to my bones, and I keep forgetting to breathe with the anticipation of it.

By the time he's traveled the length of me twice, I can't wait for him do it again with less clothes. My heart is beating so hard I can hear it in my ears, and my throat is so dry I keep swallowing.

"You look thirsty." Hunter offers me some water.

I've never been this parched. I sit up and gulp it. I eye him over the top of the bottle, there on his knees in front of me. He's taken off his glasses and he stares back at me, intent on his project. Waiting for me to be ready.

"You gotta hydrate," he murmurs.

When I reach for him, intending to map him in return, he shakes his head and asks if he can remove one of my layers. My fingers tremble when I hand the water bottle back.

He unbuttons my jeans and slides them down my legs gently, and the rough denim feels like sandpaper scratching across my overly sensitized skin. I crave his touch at this point. I ache for it.

I've had hook-ups where I felt embarrassed when I took off my clothes, uncertain of my curvy body or my body hair routine. Not with Hunter. There is no judgment in his touch, just a hunger to learn. When he runs his fingers up my thighs, he takes in their contour without shame. This is my body; this is the scenic route he takes to see more of me.

When he touches me, running his palms up over my calves, my knees, my thighs, there's a gush of warmth at my core. Holy shit, I'm not sure I've ever been this ready for someone before they've ever touched me there. Imagining Hunter's fingers thrust inside me makes me close my eyes and moan. I stretch my arms up above my body and luxuriate in the fact this man knows how to orienteer my body. When was the last time I didn't have to lead a man by the hand to the places that would make me scream for him? I thought that was simply the burden of being a woman: having to draw a map for every man I slept with. Now, here is Hunter, drawing a map without help from me. Finding his way to places I hadn't even thought to show him.

Hunter spreads my legs and rubs up my inner thighs, over my pantied mound, tickling the sides of my belly, then over my bra-covered breasts again. Sessioning me. Running the same—what did they call the rock formations in the trail?—*features* to gain familiarity and figure out a plan for success.

I'm dying to know Hunter's plan for my breasts. And elsewhere.

"Can we..." I pluck at my bra, wanting to take it off. Hunter helps me, reaching around my back to unhook it. He does it so easily, his nimble fingers working the bra like he would any other gear. Then the cool air hits my bare breasts and I shiver.

"Cold?" he asks.

"Your hands are warm."

So he covers my breasts with them. Now he knows the shape of them, the gentle slopes and valley between. He traces lines up and down and blows on their highest elevation, making pebbles of my nipples. He tugs on the peaks, making sparks shoot down my body to my toes.

He helps me lift my hips to pull my panties down, and at last scoots me up the bed so my feet are no longer on the floor. Then he turns to mapping new terrain—the folds between my legs. He doesn't need a guide there, either. He nuzzles into me, parts my flesh with his fingers, and doesn't hesitate.

Only in my wildest dreams did I imagine Hunter using his

tongue to trace my core, taking the scenic route up and down over my clit before dipping deep inside. Something gives way for him, my hips straining to press into his hold, my core calling out for more.

"Fuck," I gasp, and put my hands on his shoulders which are still fully dressed. I push on his shirt, blindly demanding in my eagerness for skin against skin, and Hunter relents and pulls back to undress.

He undresses, revealing bulging biceps and shoulders cut like granite. I knew Hunter was fit, from his job and his lifestyle. His muscles aren't from the gym. He has a soft belly but sculpted thighs. His cock, hard and strong as the rest of him, bobs in my direction when he takes off his boxer briefs.

He comes to me when I reach for him with both hands, greedy for him. I slide my hands over his body, knowing I'm not skilled enough—or patient enough—to learn him the way he did me. Not right now. Not when I'm leaking all over his bed from the need to have him between my legs.

Combing my hands through his loose hair as it falls over his shoulder, something animalistic takes over and I arch my back, pulling his head down to my breast. He laves my nipple, his hair tickling me. I take fists full of it. I part my legs as wide as I can and the tip of his cock almost slips inside of me.

Finally, Hunter takes mercy on me and gets a condom from his nightstand. "Are you ready?" he asks. He climbs up my geography and holds himself over me, braced on both hands.

"I can't wait any longer," I moan, raising my knees up around his hips.

When he enters me, it's what I imagine summiting a mountain must be like. I gasp a deep breath and open for him, ready for this new adventure.

Hunter is as ready as I am, spearing me deeply with his hard length. We rut together, finding our rhythm, sweat gliding between our skin. The angles of his body above, against, inside mine are miraculous. We are perfect together.

He reaches between us and rubs my clit, and that's all it takes for me to take off, soaring above our bodies for one out-of-body moment of climax. While I'm there, I watch Hunter come inside my body, his face a mask of bliss.

He collapses on top of me for only a moment before he hops up and runs away naked. I blink around in confusion and he's back quickly with a washcloth and a flannel robe that he helps me into. He directs me to the bathroom and then curls around me, tucking the robe close around my legs, and holding me as I enjoy the remnants of my orgasm.

"You OK?" he murmurs against the back of my neck. I nod, shivering as his whiskers rub my neck. He tucks the plaid blanket on his bed closer around me, and then I stare at the map tacked to Hunter's wall as he starts to snore behind me.

Well, *shit*. I can't ignore the way Hunter revealed so much of who he is during sex, nor the way pieces of me connected to pieces of him as more than *just* sex. We fit together. I didn't expect that. He was like a puzzle piece that completed my map. And the aftercare—the way he made sure I was comfortable, warm and clean after—was a big part of that.

I can't deny it now. This man is more than a summer fling for me.

eleven

HUNTER

MOLLIE and her friends will be at the bar, and they'll be talking about me. I know these things like facts. So I'm reluctant to go out with Scott and Tyler. I do anyway, hungry for more time with Mollie and, OK, yes, more information.

Am I merely part of her "summer adventure story" or is there more to this?

They're at a hotel rooftop bar in the middle of the main strip of town. We're only about four stories up, as high as buildings in Telluride get, but it's still open-air. The air is crisp, having cooled down after sunset. The women are wearing jackets. Tyler brought Zoe, who I recognize immediately by her signature red scarf.

Sophie, who is apparently about to move to a state where weed is illegal, is asking Zoe about her vape pen. Scott is flirting with Nora, as usual. And Mollie is asking Tyler why he moved to Telluride—making him shift foot to foot.

"I retired sort of abruptly and needed a change," he says, a line I've heard him use before when he's trying to get out of this topic of conversation. I come up behind him and clap him on the back.

"Hi, Mollie," I say, without moving closer. I'm pretty sure we're not in a "greet each other with a kiss hello" relationship.

Her smile up at me makes me wonder. "Hi, Hunter." We stare at each other for a beat too long, and Tyler looks between us with eyebrows raised.

"Um," Mollie goes on. "I was asking Tyler why Telluride? I mean, it's gorgeous. But it's so small and doesn't it get snowed in during the winter?"

"We get plenty of snow here," I agree. Of course the idea of living in Telluride sounds ridiculous to a city girl. I try to ignore the twinge from her criticism—it's a reminder she won't stay. "Does anybody need another drink?"

"You sit down," Tyler says quickly, taking the opening I left him. "I'll get us all a round."

Tyler is one of those people who came to Telluride to escape. He doesn't *mind* being cut off from the rest of the world. That was one of his goals, as a man who once appeared on many front pages and TV news programs. He doesn't like explaining that to strangers, either.

I sit down on the bench beside Mollie and she smiles at me. Again, it crosses my brain that she's waiting for a more robust greeting. I'm not sure, so the moment passes. "Have you ever lived anywhere else? Or are you addicted to the adventures?" she asks.

"Yes, nailed it." I reply, even though it's not quite that easy. She's right that living in Telluride isn't easy, even as a local. It's hard to find sustainable work and housing here. "At first it was just seasonal work, from back when I was a teen. I actually started as a ski instructor. And then I met Tom and started helping during shoulder season. Eventually, he was able to offer me a year-round job. It made sense. I'm lucky. I get to do work I love full-time."

"It can't pay very well, though, right?" Nora sits down on Mollie's other side and Scott crashes onto the bench beside me.

"Do you need a drink?" Scott asks me. Now it's my turn to be saved by a friend. Obviously, I don't like talking about my salary or how little I'm saving for the future. Or how my body will eventually give out and I'll be out of work, much like Tyler—who at least had a more lucrative career before that happened.

"Tyler's getting them," Mollie says.

"I'm going to see if he needs help," I say, hopping up.

The question I'm running away from is a fair one. And Nora's probably making sure her friend doesn't get any long-term ideas about "a fling."

Standing at the bar with Tyler, I glance back at them. Nora and Mollie are laughing at something Scott said. Scott and Nora's flirtation is clearly so flimsy it will blow away by the end of the week. And that's probably what Mollie wants from me, too. I *know* it's what Nora and Sophie want from me for their friend. I'm really trying to be that for Mollie—if only so I can spend more time with her.

It would be easier if I was that kind of guy. The kind I look like to them: the happy-go-lucky, not-worried-about-tomorrow kind of guy. The truth is, I worry constantly. *How late is too late to start a 401k? What skills am I building that I can lean on in the future? Who am I going to grow old with?*

It won't be Mollie. She's leaving at the end of the week. But instead of telling myself I'm wasting my time with her, I'm greedy for the time we have. I wish we were alone right now, instead of in this crowd.

"You've got it bad, huh?" Tyler says, startling me out of my staring contest with the future I can't have.

"Oh, um…"

Shrugging, he hands me two pint glasses. "I'm not going to tell you to be careful. Sometimes something unexpected turns into the most fun you ever had. Maybe you should go with the flow. For once."

Go with the flow. Tyler's words dance inside me as my eyes meet Mollie's. For a moment the rest of the bar disappears and all I see is how her entire face brightens with her big smile. A big smile that feels like it's only meant for me. "Yeah, I'm good at that."

Pulling me back into the conversation, Tyler smirks. "Think of it like a river you're navigating. You have to go with the current. Plus, steering around obstacles can be the best part."

"Is Mollie the river in this metaphor?"

"Mollie's in the boat with you, man."

Following Tyler back to the table, I wonder about his advice. *Is* Mollie in this with me? Watching her raise her head and smile at me again as I come nearer, I want to believe she is. After only a few days knowing her, I'm not sure and I don't know how I'd ask.

"You two are so cute," Sophie says. "Stop pretending you're not super into each other."

Mollie and I freeze.

"This isn't high school; you don't have to update your social media status," Sophie goes on. "We get it. You're in a situation-ship. It's fine. You're allowed to touch."

I sit back down beside Mollie, carefully *not* touching her. I don't know what she wants here. Am I supposed to deny it?

"We're the ones who told you to have some fun this week!" Nora adds.

"Well, in that case," Scott says, and switches sides on the bench to sit so close to Nora he's practically in her lap. She laughs and shoves at him.

"Yeah, we're...yeah." Mollie bites her lip.

So I put my arm around her. After all, I want what I can have while it's here.

She tucks in under my arm like she's cold, and holds the hand that's draped over her shoulder.

"Awww," coos our group of friends. Then they turn back to their various distractions. Like it's no big deal, what just happened. Like we didn't declare ourselves in the middle of a fucking tragedy.

My body relaxes involuntarily with Mollie pressed up against me, despite the torrent of emotions ripping me up inside. This feels like where I'm supposed to be, even though I know our future. But I like the feel of her in my arms too much to protect myself from the pain.

* * *

I've decided Mollie needs a chance to enjoy riding the bike, so the next day I take her on a flat gravel trail without any features. I watch her as closely as I can while we go down the trail, single-file in some places, and catch her smiling more than gritting her teeth in concentration like she did when we were mountain biking the other day.

I like seeing her happy when we're together.

Unfortunately, the weather doesn't cooperate. It's sunny and warm in the morning when we set out, but rain clouds roll in around the time we stop for lunch. It doesn't sound like a thunderstorm, so I find us a pair of large trees to shelter under.

How do I tell Mollie it's OK for her to enjoy this kind of ride more than the other one without sounding patronizing? I try asking, "Was this ride more fun than the last one?"

She laughs. "Thanks for taking it easy on me."

"Well, it's less technical, but a long ride like this probably takes more endurance. You're getting in a great workout for your heart."

"You always have a positive spin."

Shaking my head, I survey her, noting she's not quite meeting my eyes. "You don't have to be good at everything."

"I'm in no danger of that!"

The way I see Mollie is, she's brave. She doesn't pick things up easily and she knows it, yet she's willing to try anything—and keep trying when she doesn't succeed. It's not something I see much, working with men who have muscle memory for basically any athletic activity and mostly gave up on anything else. Tom has more or less stopped doing math—because he's not good at it—something that alarms me every time I see his paperwork. He keeps track of income and expenses on two separate spreadsheets that rarely see each other. And won't let me streamline the system. It's how he avoids beating himself up for what's not going well.

Unlike Tom, Mollie dives in whether she thinks it will go well or not.

"I think it's great that you don't mind being bad at some things."

She makes a face at me. "Gee, thanks."

"I mean..." I rub at the nap of my neck. "It's hard. To admit you're not good at something. And then to keep doing it."

"The definition of insanity? Expecting a different outcome?"

"It's also OK if you want to stop. You don't have to do all the activities this week, you know. If you're not enjoying it. We don't even have to keep axe-throwing."

"I like axe-throwing with you," is all she says.

"You're not just saying that because..." I pause, reluctant to inadvertently criticize her.

"Because?" She looks at me. She sniffs, her nose likely running as the sweat evaporates off our bodies.

"Well, because it's what I want to do. I don't want to be like your friends, getting you to do things you don't really want to do all the time."

She makes a face and looks away. I'm worried I annoyed her with my inability to keep my thoughts to myself. My *worries* to myself.

"It's not that," she says. "I might not be axe-throwing if it wasn't for Nora and Sophie, or I might not *still* be axe-throwing if not for you. But I like that. I like getting the chance to do something I wouldn't normally do because of the people I can do it with. It's sort of a luxury to keep going back over and over. My friends in Denver would give up after one try. And I'd decide I was bad at it and never go back again."

"You could spend a lot of time only doing things once," I observe. Most of the people who come on our adventure tours do that. They try things once, decide they know enough about it, and probably spend the rest of their lives talking about that one time they did it.

"I'm kind of tired of that shallow life," Mollie says, so quietly I almost can't hear her over the rain. "I could stand to go deep on a few more things."

And then it starts pouring. I don't think the afternoon shower will last long, but it's turned the air chilly and Mollie and I are both wearing summer clothes—padded shorts and light jerseys. I can't believe I didn't pack rain jackets. Of course it's going to rain in Telluride in the afternoon. But they weren't in my pack.

I offer her my arm to nestle under for warmth and she does without hesitation. We stand under the trees, shivering and looking out at the puddles forming, and I wonder if she feels the same way I do: that we're lucky.

Last night, I started reading a book about the art of letting go. It says that knowing you can't hold onto something can make it seem even more precious—and that in itself is a good reason to be willing to let go. Holding on can be a hindrance, the book claims.

Even though it's not going to last, in this moment, I wouldn't want to be anywhere except right here with Mollie. She's putting out heat next to me, which probably means she's freezing, but she's smiling out at the weather. And she's holding onto me.

Maybe, if this were forever, it wouldn't feel as good to me.

This is something *I'm* not good at: enjoying a moment that won't come again. Damn if I'm not going to try.

* * *

The Trouble Trio are trying to convince Mollie not to be nervous about the overnight stay in the woods.

"Well, when was the last time *you* spent the night on the ground?" She finally asks, logically. "In bear country?"

"Oh come on, we don't have to worry about bears." Standing safely in the lobby of the adventure center, one of the guys looks completely confident in his incorrect statement.

"We are definitely camping in bear country," I volunteer. "That's why we're bringing a bear can."

"A bear can?" repeats Sophie, sounding doubtful.

The guy trying to score with Mollie puffs up. "They're more scared of us than we are of them."

"That might be true, but when there's food involved, it changes the equation," I say. I've given this spiel a hundred times. I look around to ensure everyone else in the lobby is listening. I've caught their attention by talking about bears, an animal most of them would have never seen outside a zoo. "The most important thing is to keep the bears from associating food with humans. That is dangerous for both us and them."

I sit them all down in front of the laptop I set up in the lobby and have them watch one of the educational videos my friend Valentine made. It teaches about bear safety, and since it's fast-paced and cut for social media, it's fun to watch.

It's only an overnight trip. We'll drive deep enough into the mountains not to hear highway traffic and then walk a few miles, in a loop that will bring us directly back to the car the next day. We'll see an alpine lake and a waterfall on the trip, as an incentive. But it's an easy trail with mild elevation gain and we'll be back tomorrow.

Still, Scott and I prepare like we're going to war.

Besides the bear can, the most important thing I'm bringing on this trip is pain meds. I know from experience there's going to be a lot of complaining about the weight of the backpacks and the miles we're putting in—even though we set a slow pace.

I look over at Scott, who rattles a bottle he's putting in his bag at me. I grin and rattle mine back.

I'd like to catch a moment or two alone with Mollie this trip. Maybe take her up above the waterfall, where we don't usually take the group for fear of eroding the trail with too many feet. I haven't talked to Scott about it, worried he'll tease me for breaking the rules. I've warned him before to put distance between himself and women on these trips, where they might feel the forced proximity like a threat. It would be fair for him to remind me of that advice.

Mollie had asked me if we could share a tent and I had to tell her I didn't think it was a good idea. But I liked that she'd asked.

When we head out, everyone is in a cheerful mood. Sophie, Nora, and the 20-something Trouble Trio whose names seem interchangeable are rowdy in the back of the van we drive to the trailhead.

Within two hours into the back country hike, there are complaints. They're the usual ones about the weight of the bags, even though Scott and I are carrying more than our share of the weight for the trip. And there are doubts about the elevation gain, which is gradual but steady. I remind everyone of the beautiful lake we'll see later today. "It's an alpine lake. It's above tree line."

When no one is looking, I check in with Mollie. She's been quiet so far on the hike. "Feeling OK? No hot spots in your shoes? How's the bag fitting?"

She shakes her head, eyes on her feet. "I'm OK. Ready to get there."

"We have another couple of hours," I warn her. "Let me know if you need a break."

She nods. She acts determined to tough it out, which worries me. Complainers are annoying, but at least they're not going to suffer in silence. The quiet ones are the ones who let blisters form that prevent them from walking or sneak food into their tent that attracts wildlife.

I would be checking on Mollie either way, and this tells me something about her. She'll tough it out even when she knows better.

Even more reason for me to keep our relationship—or whatever it is—light. I don't want her to feel trapped in a relationship she's only in for the sake of her friends. I don't want her to make bad decisions while suffering in silence.

Scott is leading, so I do a count and check on the stragglers at the back of the group. Nora and Sophie, surprisingly strong hikers, are keeping up with Scott. The boys still trying to impress them are marching along at the front of the group, too. A mom and one of the teenagers are at the back. I offer them some encouragement and offer to take something out of their bags to lighten the load. They both refuse.

Bringing up the rear of the party, I spend some time thinking about how to get some alone time with Mollie that isn't irresponsible.

Everyone forgets about their complaints, at least for a moment, when we get to the lake. It glows blue from the glacier melt and the sun hitting it perfectly in the late afternoon.

"Can we set up camp here?" asks the mom. Someone always wants to know this at this point in the trip.

Some of the guys start taking off their bags.

"We can't camp here," I warn. "It's too exposed and no one can poop this close to the lake."

"Eww," a chorus responds.

Scott laughs and I shrug. "That's the reality." I glance at Mollie to see if she finds my earthy topics gross, but she's simply listening. She hasn't taken her backpack off.

One of the other women has an expression like something horrible has dawned on her. "Are there bathrooms where we're camping?" Apparently, someone didn't read the literature we gave them. Valentine has another video on this topic I should have showed them.

Smirking, Scott just his chin at me to answer. "There are no bathrooms out here. And we need to pack it out, so we have wag bags and a shovel."

Several people groan.

"We really are on an adventure," Mollie murmurs. I like her even more in this moment.

We eventually make it to our planned camp site and start setting up. Some of the guys need help setting up their tents or pounding in stakes, but don't ask for it, which is why Scott and I carry extra stakes to use once participants have bent theirs beyond use. We let them work out their frustration for a while and help people who will accept it. People like Mollie, who quietly asks me whether she needs her rain fly or can keep it off, so she can look out at the stars once it gets dark.

"I recommend you put it on." My mouth drags down. "We might get a shower and it helps with insulation. Also..." I lower my voice and peer around to make sure nobody is listening. "This way, if you sneak out of your tent in the middle of the night and come to mine, nobody will be able to tell you're not in there."

She smiles. And puts on the rain fly.

We cook soup for dinner and pass around crusty bread. It's one of the easier meals to make and carry on a short, one-night trip that's still warm and comforting. A couple of people brought their own freeze-dried meals that they abandon in favor of real food. A few people complain about the lack of a campfire, even though we've told them over and over that there's a drought.

After, I give them all the spiel—again—about locking up *all* the food and changing into different clothes to sleep in. I know a few of them are freaked out by the thought of bears entering our camp in the dark, and I let them worry about the unlikely event. Better than being too casual about putting food away.

I try to give Mollie a conspiratorial look before she climbs into her tent, and it's ruined by the headlamps we're both wearing. I end up shining my light into her eyes, which she ducks away from. "Sorry," I whisper, wincing.

Before climbing into my own tent, I check in with Scott. He walked the perimeter of the camp site and double checked the bear can. We counted everyone getting into their tents for the night. Everything's safe enough for us to close our eyes.

"Noticed you set up your tent pretty close to Mollie's," he comments wryly as we look up at the sky, darker and more full of stars than the one over town.

"Coincidence," I shrug.

"Sure," he says, a smirk in his voice, before he leaves me to turn in.

Slipping into my tent, at first I hesitate over zipping the flaps closed. My phone has no service out here, so I can't text to ask

Mollie whether she's coming. I climb into my sleeping bag and listen. The camp is quiet, still.

It's a little chilly with the tent open to the elements, so I reach to close it right as I hear the sound of a tent nearby unzipping. It's hard to tell whether it's coming from the direction of Mollie's. It could easily be someone else, already needing a pee.

A minute later, someone pulls at the flap of my tent. My heart stops for a second, the darkness and all the talk of bears getting to me. Then, against the gentle starlight, I make out the outline of Mollie. She throws her sleeping bag in, squeezes into the tent beside me, and zips it up behind her.

"Hi," she whispers, so soft I almost can't hear her even though her face is right next to mine.

"Hi." I match her quietness.

"Is this still OK?" she asks, pausing with her hand still on the zipper. "I can try to leave before anyone else gets up. Do you think you'll wake up first?"

"I usually do." Her warm breath against my lips is making me hard. I can't stop it. My dick seems to think that a tent surrounded by other people is the perfect place to have sex. "I'm glad you're here."

Tomorrow will bring more complaints and a return to the real world, but right now that all seems far away. Mollie and I are in our own bubble, where nothing can reach us.

"It's cold," she murmurs, biting her lip. "Colder than I expected."

"Get in and turn over," I whisper, trying to overcome her second-guessing.

She zips herself into her sleeping bag and turns her back to me so I can spoon her the best I can, still cocooned in my own bag. I long for the feel of her skin against mine. Instead, I rest my cheek on the cold, plastic-y lining. She kisses the hand that's holding close to her chest.

When she bumps her butt into my groin, snuggling closer to me, even with the layers between us, I smile. I like the closeness of this tent and the quietness all around us. I even like that we can't do much more than hold each other. This intimacy is more than I'm used to on a hiking trip. I could get used to it.

But I shouldn't.

After a few minutes like that, and as I'm almost drowsy enough to sleep, she breaks the silence.

"How do people fall asleep out here?" she asks softly. "It's so quiet."

I snuffle against the back of her neck. "That's one of the things people like about it."

"No, I know...OK, please don't judge me, but I usually have music or TV on when I fall asleep."

Snorting, I snuggle her closer to me. "Does it help to think about all the animals out there living their lives, just beyond this tent? It's like a wildlife soap opera out there."

"Um, no. That doesn't help me to think about animals *right outside* our flimsy tent," she hisses.

"Do you need a distraction? I think we've established you're very reward-motivated. Maybe I can help."

She stills. "What do you have in mind?"

"Well," I whisper, slowly easing the zipper on her sleeping bag open. "Is this too cold?"

She shakes her head, the wisps of her hair brushing against my nose.

It takes some quiet maneuvering, some muted grunting followed by checking in with each other that our limbs are in comfortable positions, until I can get my arm deep into her sleeping bag.

It's hot inside, pressed close against her skin. My nose is up against her neck, under her hair, where despite the rigors of the day I still get the scent of coconut.

I wiggle my hand down toward her core, Mollie shifting her body around to help me get there. I don't need the help; I memorized the map of her the other day. It's forever stored in my mind—the curve of her hip and the feel of the soft tuft of hair along her pussy filed with important things like the best route to summit Mt. Sneffels and how to change a tire.

My hand traces the route now, in the darkness of the tent, finding its way to where she's already wet for me. I listen to her short breaths and can feel her chest moving under my arm. "I bet you're not thinking about the wildlife now," I murmur into the shell of her ear, causing her to emit a slight gasp. A bear could pass right outside our tent and so long as it didn't stick its nose inside, neither of us would care.

We're both silent, only the slide back and forth of my shirt on the vinyl material of her sleeping bag hinting at the thrusting I'd like to be doing. I'm so hard, she may be able to feel me poking her in the back despite the double padding between us.

I've never had sex in a tent before. I can smell the arousal, trapped in this close space with us.

Kissing her neck, biting a little, whining softly against her skin, I rub her little nub of nerves and flex and bend my fingers so that I can reach into her. Her tiny gasps are muted, an attempt to keep this between us, and I love that. As much as I love hearing her loudly moan for me, I love hearing her keep us quiet too. I want it all with Mollie.

Desperately, I want her hands on me right now, but this is so good too. I can taste the way the skin of her neck is growing hotter. I can feel her clit swelling. Her breasts are heaving against my arm.

When she comes, she goes rigid and then collapses against me. I carefully pull my hand back out of her pants and her sleeping bag, shaking off the tightness. Instead of bringing my fingers to my mouth, I roll onto my back and shove my hand down my own sleeping bag, using the slickness of my hand to try to bring myself some relief.

Mollie, cocooned in her bag, huffs as she rolls over. Once her chin is tucked between my neck and shoulder, she whispers, "Let me do that." And shoves her hand down my front.

"Fuck," I hiss—too loudly. I try to remember who our nearest neighbor is, and then I'm distracted by Mollie's soft, cold hand around my dick. She runs her fingers up and down my shaft, then around the hair at the base. She grasps me, taking the weight of me in her hand. Then she does it again.

She's mapping me, I realize. The way I did her. She's taking time to learn my body, and I give her what she needs: I softly respond to her exploration, releasing huffs of breath when her curious fingers go somewhere I particularly like. I close my eyes and let her feel her way, using her hand to tug and swirl, running a finger over the sensitive head, making me swell even further in my pants.

It doesn't take long.

I come inside my underwear like a teenager, and thank goodness I brought an extra pair on this overnight trip because I'm going to need them.

She curls up against me, tucked into her bag, and "hmms" softly in my ear. "I think I can sleep now."

"Hmm..." Words are too difficult for me.

She drifts off quickly, her breath growing even against my neck. Now I'm the one thinking about how quiet it is between us and how there are more and more words being left unsaid.

twelve

MOLLIE

AFTER A LONG, hot shower to get the camping trip off me, all I really want is to crawl into bed. But Nora and Sophie told everyone tomorrow's my birthday, and also invited themselves along on my axe-throwing date with Hunter. And I hate to miss any time with Hunter—it's so limited.

When I woke up this morning to the gentle way he rubbed my shoulders and encouraged me to consciousness so I could crawl back to my tent before anyone else woke up, for those first few sleepy moments I imagined it was the first morning of many. Hunter and I, waking up like this. Hunter and I, whispering together at night before we both fall asleep.

Briefly, I thought we were at the beginning of a long journey together. I went back to my tent and cried softly to myself for a few minutes, with no one around to see. It's not that I've never faced heartbreak before. It's that this one seems so unnecessary. Who am I to travel to the middle of nowhere and meet the man of my dreams?

Anyway, my friends tell me I need to squeeze the last bit of juice out of my 20s.

Everyone else shows up when we get to the axe-throwing place—Scott, Tyler, Zoe, and even Tom. Hunter acts a little different when Tom is around, stiffer and less aware of me. So I'm not thrilled to see him—or any of them, turning me into the center of attention.

Their presence does apparently mean free drinks. The owner of the axe-throwing alley comes out with a pitcher of draft beer, shouting, "I hear we have a birthday!"

"Dirty 30!" Nora cheers.

And then Tom pulls out a box of assorted pastries. "These are from Dorothy. I stopped by before the cafe closed and she gave me everything she was going to throw out. No offense, Mollie. She also sent along a cupcake for you."

He lights a single candle on top of the cupcake and everyone in the venue sings before I blow it out. It's incredibly embarrassing and also really nice. I can't remember the last birthday I had where a group of friends got together and sang to me. I was probably a kid.

Let this birthday be the beginning of a decade where I really live, I wish silently. My 20s were full of trying to live up to who people wanted me to be—my mom, my friends, even myself. Now I'm ready to be a grown up who knows who she is and isn't afraid of that reality.

Sharing two lanes, we all line up and throw axes. I am by far the worst at it. Even Nora and Sophie hit the target most of the time. My axes are still going wide, not sticking, or landing on the outside edge. At least I still feel like a bad ass every time I pick up an axe; that's what keeps me going.

That and the way Hunter asks every time before he puts his hands on me to adjust my form.

Tom, who has not stopped refilling his plastic cup since he

got here, finally asks about it. "Aren't you two dating? She's probably OK with you touching her, Hunter."

Tyler and Scott both guffaw.

Behind me, Hunter's skin goes hot after the comment. I know he's not thrilled that his boss thinks he's "dating" me. Hunter's need to impress Tom—to show him he can do more—reminds me of me. If Tom doesn't think he's a professional, he certainly won't give him more responsibility.

"Consent is important," Hunter says stiffly.

"Aww," coo Nora and Sophie.

"Why hasn't someone scooped this guy up yet?" Sophie murmurs to Nora, at the same time Tom is protesting that he believes in consent, too.

"Because he lives in a remote town and works a seasonal job," Nora replies dryly.

"Oh, right."

Hunter's job isn't seasonal, though. He and Scott are the only employees Tom keeps on year-round. Hunter told me Tom can't afford more than that. If I told them that, I'd probably have to tell them they work just under the minimum that would require Tom to provide them benefits. And they'd be appalled. I was shocked when Hunter mentioned it. He added that Tom's insurance would cover things like accidents. "I'm not totally reckless," he insisted.

Of course, I know Hunter is far from reckless. Still, Sophie and Nora might not see him the way I do.

"Mollie, does Hunter need to ask every time he helps your form?" Tom is still trying to make his point.

"It's fine, Hunter," I tell him, trying to smooth things over.

Scott laughs. "Mollie, would *I* need to ask before every time I corrected your form?"

I make a face at him. Of course he would. I like Scott, but I don't want his hands on me. Especially right now, when he's half-way drunk and trying to start trouble. Nora is laughing at him, encouraging him to keep going.

"It's OK, you know," Tom announces then. "I know you boys date around. It makes sense you would meet people while working."

While I'm watching Scott exchange a smirk with Tyler, I catch Hunter's grimace out of the corner of my eye.

"In fairness, I'm only dating the one girl," Tyler offers. "And we didn't meet on the job."

"I worry about other things with you," Tom says, mouth quirking.

"Hey! Like what?"

"And I don't worry about Hunter dating a nice young woman who went on one of my tours," Tom continues, ignoring Tyler. He looks at Hunter and claps him on the back, swaying into him a little. "You're a good kid, Hunter. Don't do anything I wouldn't do."

"That doesn't leave very much off the list," Scott teases.

Tom nods and wipes his brow. "That's true. But I don't have to tell you not to do anything *Hunter* wouldn't do, now do I?"

Scott snorts. "You mean, like *anything* fun?"

"No seriously, like what?" Tyler insists, returning to the topic.

Tom turns to him and starts to explain or soothe him, but I ignore them in favor of Hunter, who whispers in my ear, "Are you ready to go?"

Nora, Sophie, and Scott are starting the dance party portion of the evening. The owner is gathering up axes and hurriedly putting them away. "Yes, definitely," I say.

We go back to Hunter's room at Tom's place. With the house empty, I wander around a little more than I did last time. There are Uncrustables in the freezer and a lot of different kinds of deli meat in the fridge. The pantry is full of trail mix and peanut butter. The bathroom smells a bit like a wet dog, and there's a book about orienteering on the back of the toilet.

"Are you done exploring?" Hunter asks when I join him in his bedroom. He's stretched out on his bed reading a book, and puts a bookmark at his place when he looks up at me. I wonder if this is what it'd be like if we lived together: me always catching Hunter with a book. I like the way he looks, relaxed and unconcerned about me being nosy.

"For now," I tease. "It's funny—it's easy to tell what stuff is yours versus the other guys."

"You think?"

"You can test me later." I climb onto the bed and stretch out parallel to him. He smiles at me and moves some hair off my face that's fallen there. "What are you reading?" I dip the cover of the book he's holding toward me. It's called *The Art of Letting Go*.

"It's a book about rewiring your brain."

"Hmm…Is it working?"

His smile is a little sad. "I don't think so."

"Well, that's pretty hard to do. What needs rewiring exactly?"

"Oh, my worries about the future, I guess. My asking questions like…what happens next? And what does this mean." He strokes the back of my hand where it rests on the bed between us.

"Those all seem normal to me." Those same questions are on almost constant repeat in my own head. About Hunter, about life. Are we actually going to talk about *us*? I'm not sure I'm ready. That conversation may lead to talking about our ending, and I don't think I'm ready for this to end yet.

"Normal," he agrees, gaze skipping past mine to the other side of the room. "And maybe not helpful."

I nod and flop onto my back. His pillow smells like him. Like the outdoors and some kind of harsh soap. "Do you worry about things like your job?"

"Yeah," he agrees, leaning over me to put the book on the floor by his bed. "I worry about how long I can do it and what I will do after I can't anymore." He stays like that, half resting on me and half on the bed beside me. I like the weight of him over my body, the sense of safety it gives me.

"What did you want to be when you grew up?" I ask him.

"A cowboy." He smiles. "And I kind of am now, in some ways. Still, when you're a kid, you don't think about all the problems that come with a career, do you?"

"No kidding. I wanted to be a coffee shop owner."

"Like Dorothy?"

"Yes, exactly like Dorothy. Then I learned about profit margins and overhead. And discovered having a cat in your cafe is a health violation and giving away food is taking money out of your own pocket."

He laughs. "Was that your vision? A cat and giveaways?"

"That's how Barbie always did it." I grin back at him. "She always had time for other hobbies, somehow, too."

"So you became a paralegal instead?"

"Yeah." I feel defensive, even though Hunter's question wasn't particularly probing. He's tracing his fingers up and down my torso, making my insides turn to water. "It's stable and didn't take much extra school."

"And do you have time for hobbies?"

"What hobbies. I don't have hobbies." My hobbies are brunch on Sundays and sleeping as late as I possibly can. My life back home is boring in the worst way: it lacks inspiration.

"Well, now you do. You have to keep up your axe-throwing."

I imagine inviting my friends in Denver to go axe-throwing. They'd go once, I'm sure. Mostly to drink and post on social media that they were there. No one would take it as seriously as Hunter does. "Yeah." I sigh.

"Where did your mind go just then?" Hunter asks, brushing his fingertip down my hairline. "You looked all sad."

Of course he noticed. I can't say, "I'm going to miss you." So I reply, "I was thinking about dreams. And goals. And how I don't really have any as an adult."

He shakes his head. He carefully moves more hair off my face, laying each strand gently on the pillow beside my head as if each piece has nerves. "That's not true. When you wake up in the morning, how do you want to feel?"

Taking a deep breath, I close my eyes and think about my first thought when I usually open them. I usually wake to an alarm and the tension of knowing I have to get up and accomplish so much before I go sit at my desk for the rest of the day. "At peace," I say finally.

"I read a book once that said happiness is making decisions that align the most with your values. Being at peace might be the same as happiness, defined that way."

Opening my eyes, I imagine Hunter's face being the first thing I see in the morning and what that would feel like. "Huh. What do you want when you first wake up in the morning?"

He smiles. "Other than breakfast?"

Shoving him a little without actually pushing off me, I protest, "Hey, we were having a serious moment!"

"Yeah, I know. But I think I want the same thing. I mean, I want adventure. I also want to come back to my room and be able to open a book and disappear into it. I want to know there's a peaceful space waiting for me at the end of the day."

A vision comes to me of Hunter curled up at the end of a day with a book—maybe after showering, the ends of his hair still wet—and me snuggling up against him, his nook my pillow. I squirm a little, burrowing into the picture.

"You cold?" he asks, and starts to pull the blanket up around me.

"No, just ticklish," I answer, which of course leads to him tickling me in earnest. I hope the house is still empty, because my giggling gets loud.

The feeling of Hunter above me is so intoxicating—on top of already being a little tipsy from this night—I forget to keep laughing and nuzzle into his skin. He slides his body down mine, rumpling my clothes, and starts unbuttoning my pants.

"You don't have to..." I begin, expecting little resistance to my out.

"Are you kidding?" he says. "I'm exploring."

I put my hand back down on the bed. "I support your adventures."

"Yes. That's something I like about you." He smiles up at me. And I can't believe I somehow found myself the adventure this man wants to go on.

Then he dives in, touching his lips to parts of me that have been neglected by most of the men I've slept with before. It's not popular anymore, this heady dive into a woman's core. At least according to brunch conversations with friends.

Hunter makes it exactly what he said: an exploration, his tongue reaching deep inside me, his lips running up my center. My job is to let him map the inside of me. To open for his probing fingers, to respond to the gentle scrape of his face against my thigh. He feasts, learning every inch of me wringing out all the pleasure. No man has ever made me feel so wanted, like I'm the air he needs to breathe.

I come like that, my back arching away from the bed, Hunter's head between my legs. If my life were a book, I'd want this moment to be the epigraph to my 30s. The inspiration for what's to come. I hope he left a trail to find his way back again and again, because I want him to live there, nestled close to me.

When he slides inside me, I rub my entire body up the length of him, trying to cement this moment in my head. I craved this feeling last night—of Hunter's bare skin pressed against mine, of his length inside me—as though I've already grown addicted.

His scent as I tuck my nose into the spot between his neck and shoulder reminds me of the best things about winter: it's fresh and clean, like fresh snow. I bite down on the soft flesh there, unable to help myself, needing to mess up that perfection a little. Wanting to own a little bit of it for myself. He grunts against me and comes almost immediately, and now I know something about Hunter's body, too: that he likes a little possession.

There's something very different about this casual hook-up; it's nothing like encounters I've had back in the city. It's in the way Hunter knows my body so well already. The way he makes sure I'm warm after we both come. And how, even if I have to let go at the end of the week, I'll want to remember this forever.

* * *

The next morning, I wake to find Hunter snoring on his back beside me. I watch him for a little while, smiling at his unconscious ease, before I have to get up and use the bathroom.

The house is quiet. I think everyone else is still asleep, so I tiptoe to the kitchen to find some water.

Tom is sitting at the table, surrounded by maps and gear, drinking coffee. He's wearing a pair of reading glasses. "Pot's still on," he offers quietly, not even changing expression when he sees me.

"Thanks," I murmur, very aware that I'm in an awkward space between Hunter not wanting his boss to know about us and his boss knowing and not caring.

"Sit down," he adds, after I've filled a mug with coffee. It doesn't sound quite like an invitation; more an order. But almost every time I've heard Tom speak, he sounds like he's giving orders. So I hesitate.

He takes his glasses off and gestures at the table, his gaze steady on me. So I sit.

"Hunter's not as hard as he looks on paper," Tom says bluntly, not waiting for me to take my first sip. I pause with the mug held in both hands, half-way to my mouth. "He's softer than my other guys. Easier to hurt. Oh, not out on the trails. In here." Tom puts his hand over his heart.

Not sure how to respond, I nod.

"I'm a bit protective of all my guys," Tom continues. "But Hunter's special. He dedicates himself to everything he does. And everyone."

Not sure how to respond to being someone Hunter *does*, I stay silent.

"All I'm saying is, let him down easy when you go. Don't do that thing they do in the city—the 'ghosting.' Please." He makes quotation marks around the word, pursing his lips like it's dirty. I feel the same way about the practice. It dawns on me that it would be hard to ghost someone in a town as small as Telluride. You'd see them on the street or at the grocery store whether you wanted to pretend they didn't exist anymore or not.

"OK," I say. Hesitating, I add after a moment, "I can't guarantee he won't get hurt. I can't guarantee we won't both get hurt."

The older man surveys me. "That's a true statement if I ever heard one. For a city girl, you've got a good head on your shoulders."

I'm not sure if I've ever valued a compliment more than this one. Hunter's scary father figure approves of me, at least a little.

He holds up the reading glasses and shakes them at me. "Hunter does too. He's the one who told me to get these glasses, you know that? I put it off for so long and he was right, they change everything."

A good idea can change everything. The phrase lands in my head suddenly, startling me with its insistence. I don't know where that came from. It's like I woke up 30 and suddenly started giving myself inscrutable advice.

"At least you're in it together," Tom adds. He puts his glasses back on and goes back to what he was reading, seeming to dismiss me. I start to stand before his final comment, said almost to himself: "That counts for something at the end."

thirteen

HUNTER

MOLLIE TOLD me Tom saw her that morning in the house, but he doesn't act any more grumpy than usual when I meet him in the office to go over the books.

Tom hates this part of the business. Yet he won't turn it over to me, saying between the two of us non-math-majors we should be able to catch each other's errors. Which is fair, I guess. I don't have any more training in running a business than Tom does.

Still, I'm pretty sure there's something wrong with the numbers and Tom's business might not last for long if it keeps going like this.

I've tried to talk to Tom about it before and gotten a non-answer, and I try again that morning. Being with Mollie makes me think I should try harder. If I can do more than lead expeditions, I should at least give it a shot.

"Don't you worry about things you don't control, Hunter," Tom says. "You have enough going on in your life."

That's a new one. And proves that Tom seeing Mollie this

morning *did* make an impact. "I'm not distracted," I say, uncertain whether this is Tom's critique. "I can still do my job."

"But this isn't your job, is it?" Tom, sitting behind the desk, peers at me. He's wearing reading glasses. He hasn't mentioned them, or that they were my idea. I can tell they've made it easier for him to concentrate on his screen. I guess knowing I did some good is enough for me, even though I'd like some credit for helping.

Instead, I flinch away from the hardness of his tone. He's right; I'm the one sitting with a stack of papers in my lap because I don't have a desk in this office. Maybe he *is* grumpy about Mollie.

"Maybe we ought to think about that," Tom goes on. "What I'm paying you for, exactly."

A cold knot swells in my gut. Is Tom threatening to fire me? Is this because I'm sleeping with a paying client? Scott does that all the time. What makes me different?

Because I'm the responsible one.

"I'm, uh..." My mind goes blank as I try to come up with a good self-defense. "I'm a good guide." *Stellar*. I wince at my poor defense.

"I know you are," Tom replies, sorting through papers as though I'm not freaking out across from him. "You're one of the best. But you seem to have your eye on something else."

"No!" I protest, thinking he's talking about Mollie. "I mean, I can care about more than one thing at a time."

"Hm," Tom replies. Brow creased, Tom's gaze moves to his computer screen.

"Are you, is there something you're not happy about?"

"Our numbers this year..." Tom waves at the mess of papers on his desk. My heart sinks. If we're not doing well, Tom's not going to be able to keep me or Scott on full-time. "They're a little overwhelming. The new packages you came up with are selling well. I can barely keep track."

That's news Tom hasn't shared with me before now. I release a breath. Another of my ideas that's working. "You need a new system. I can help with that..."

Tom cuts me off with a wave. "I *said*, I don't pay you for that, Hunter. Keep your eyes on your actual job."

The back of my throat hurts. I swallow back the frustration and nod. You can't guide an unwilling tour, and you definitely can't teach a stubborn boss. Even if I'm pretty sure I could help.

I stand instead, saying I need to get ready for an outing, and leave Tom there to sort through his own mess. He's right on one count, anyway: I've got messes of my own to deal with.

* * *

Mollie and the others went white water rafting with Scott and Tyler while I led the group that went hiking that afternoon. Their group has already been back and put away all the gear by the time I return with my group.

Back in the house alone, I spend some time wondering where they all went before I remember the hike Scott loves to take girls he's dating on. It's near town and goes to a cave few people know about, but the route to get there is sketchy as hell. We don't take paying groups that way. Tom's insurance wouldn't cover it.

There's a bad feeling in my gut about it. I put my hiking boots back on and head back outside.

The hike runs parallel to town for most of the way, so I walk through town planning to take a short cut. I run into Zoe, coming out of the dispensary. She asks if I'm "on a mission."

"I am," I reply. "Have you seen Mollie or her friends?"

"No," she says. "No offense; we're not exactly buddies."

Sure, Zoe is not going to be hanging out with out-of-towners any time soon. She runs a rental property that has probably taught her a lot about boundaries with tourists.

"Mollie seems nice, though," she adds, notably leaving out her friends. Nora and Sophie aren't terrible. They *are* very focused on themselves.

"We're just...hanging out," I say with a sigh.

"That's how Tyler and I started, too," Zoe replies with a smile. "Now look at us. Still...hanging out." She smiles a little, the smile of a woman who isn't saying what she really wants.

We could probably have a heart-to-heart in the street and talk about our respective heartaches, but I tell Zoe I need to vaguely go check on something and she nods and waves me off.

There's an exposed water pipe that is the most direct route to the cave from town. Scott is an idiot who walked it like a tightrope once and now tries to convince anyone gullible to try it, too.

So I'm not completely shocked to see Mollie standing on it when I get close enough to see what's going on. She's frozen, her arms spread wide for balance, her feet at criss-crossed angles on the pipe. She's only a few steps out from the ground—far enough my heart skips a beat.

"What the *fuck* are you doing?" Scott, standing at the far end of the pipe, can't hear me. Nora and Sophie, who are at the safe end near me, do.

"He made it look so easy," Nora says.

Sophie's face is drawn. "And now it looks so high."

The pipe is, indeed, at least 10 feet in the air. It extends over rugged terrain that would not be easy to land on in the event of a fall.

My ears hurt from how hard my heart is pounding as I stare hard at Mollie, standing over that chasm. She looks vulnerable and alone on that pipe, her hair blowing in a light breeze and her hands wobbling as she keeps them out for balance.

"You're OK!" Scott calls back to Mollie. "You can turn around and go back if you want to!"

"I can't...move..." Mollie whispers, barely loud enough to float back to us. I can see her legs are shaking. Abandoned out on that pipe, she's stuck between committing to the plan and reversing course.

Dropping my camelbak backpack on the ground beside Mollie's friends, I walk out onto the pipe. I've never walked this before—I'm not *stupid*—and the pipe itself could be slippery, but I trust the grippy soles on my boots. Mollie's boots are new and relatively untested, aside from our hike the other day, and I don't know how sticky they are.

It doesn't take long before I am close enough to her to say, "I'm going to touch you now and help you turn around."

"OK," she says, her voice trembling.

"Don't lock your knees."

"OK," she repeats, her breath short and wheezy. "I'm not good at balance," she reminds me in a small voice.

"I remember, but I'll guide you through this. *We* got this," I say. Putting my hands on her waist, I gently pressure her to turn to the right, shuffling her feet as she goes, until she's facing me.

We look at each other and her eyes are steady. They're filled with fear, but she's not melting down. She's waiting for instructions. She trusts me to lead her. That's good.

"Now I'm going to turn around. You're going to keep one hand on my waist, only not for balance. Don't hold tight, OK? Let me turn without trying to hold onto me."

"OK," she says, her voice still faint. She loosens her fingers on my shirt, though, so I'm not worried that when I move, I'm going to unbalance her and she'll take me down with her.

Continuing to speak to her in an even tone, I turn around.

"Now we're going to walk back toward Nora and Sophie. One foot in front of the other, got it? Small steps."

"Got it," she repeats. I can feel her hand on my waist, and I don't look down. She's holding onto me loosely. I step forward, and she follows.

Moving quickly, yet not so fast I lose her, I move us back toward stable ground. I keep my eyes on the other two women, urging us on. They're waving and cheering, like encouragement can save us from this situation. The closer we get to safety, the angrier I am that we're doing this in the first place.

Mollie's hand on my waist is a steady pressure. We're going to be OK.

Once we both have two feet on firm ground, Nora and Sophie hug Mollie. "Oh my god! You could have died!"

I'm not sure either of us would have died had we fallen, but it would have hurt. A lot. Something definitely would have broken.

I glare back at Scott, on the other side. It's hard to tell at this distance, but I think he looks abashed. "You could have gotten us sued and them killed!" I yell at him, unable to keep biting my tongue.

He spreads his arms, like "what can I do about it now?" And I turn away, unable to keep looking at him.

Mollie is looking back at me now, her eyes filled with tears. Her friends both have a hand on her, like they're making sure she's real. "I know that was stupid," she says.

"It was," I reply stiffly. It's not kind, but I'm not particularly kind right now. "You don't have to try *everything*."

"I know," she whispers. Her friends glare at me.

"Town is that way." I point them in the right direction before I stomp off, leaving them there. My stomach feels like it needs to empty and my head is pounding. I've even got a tremble in my legs.

Once I'm alone, I end up pacing in my room, unable to sit

because of the buzzing beneath my skin. Tom has warned me before about judging the tourists—"sizing them up too quickly and deciding they fall into one category means they can surprise you, for good or bad," he'll say.

And I know that I can be judgmental. I'm critical of people for the very quality I see in myself: we're too fast to plan and too slow to change our opinion.

It's not that I haven't had to rescue people before. It's that this time it was Mollie. And I thought she knew better than to follow someone mindlessly.

Maybe I was wrong. Maybe she's not that different from her friends, who are encouraging her to use this week of adventure to be someone else. And maybe I'm no different than her attempt at that pipe—another "adventure" for her to share at her Sunday brunches.

fourteen

MOLLIE

NORA AND SOPHIE are unusually quiet when we get back to our hotel room. They're both remorseful over what happened, over encouraging me to "try" walking on that pipe, carried away in the moment and blind to the dangers.

My own mind is a whirl. I'm ashamed of myself for going along with whatever my friends told me to do. And right after I'd told myself I was entering a new phase in my life, too. I'd thought—now that I'm 30—I could live up to being "sweet and daring," like Hunter called me. But I'd done it again by letting someone else define what that meant *for* me, instead of listening to my own voice inside my own damn head.

I'd thought I was someone I'm not in that moment. Someone careless. Someone who can sleep with a lovely man and forget about him in a few days when she goes back to her "real" life. Someone who has a real life she cares to go back to. If one idea could change everything, I'd thought a casual near-death experience could really kickstart my thinking. How stupid.

Hunter had been so disappointed in me. Like he saw me as that different person in that moment, too.

When my mind is chaos, I always turn to my mother. She has the most orderly mind of anyone I know. She runs a newsroom that never shuts down and lots of people constantly ask her questions that depend on timing and accuracy. She knows how to triage a problem.

Stepping out on the balcony of our hotel room for privacy, I call her. After I explain the issue—trying to be succinct, as Mom always taught me—she says, "You sound like you're having a quarter-life crisis."

"What? I'm just being stupid by trying to impress a boy and my friends even though I'm old enough to know better." My mom's answers are usually not existential.

"Well, that's the immediate problem, yes," she says, as usual showing no mercy for my embarrassment. "The root of the problem, what's motivating you, is unhappiness with your life. That's obvious."

"You sound like Nora and Sophie," I grumble.

"I most certainly do not," she snaps. "They're trying to slap a bandaid on your symptoms. I'm telling you to deal with them. Sit down, make a list of everything you want from your life, and then come up with logical solutions to move forward with. This is not something you fix in a week or by sleeping with some boy you met a few days ago."

"Hey, I did meet him a few days ago, but he's not *some boy*," I protest. "He's really...he's...he's kind and he rescued me from my own stupidity. More than once. And he called me daring and he reads books to try to understand the world better. Also, he's a man."

Mom is silent for a beat longer than she ever is. She's constantly multitasking, so maybe she got distracted by something else. "Well, perhaps you put him on your list," she says finally. "Your list of things you want from your life. If not him, someone like him. That's what it sounds like you want, to me."

My mouth is dry, and not only from the lack of humidity in the Colorado air. I forgot this is what happens when I talk to my mom: she calls me out. She sees things I haven't acknowledged about myself. She senses that when I talk about Hunter, I get more excited than I've been about anything else in a long time.

"And don't seek out near-death experiences unless you're willing to deal with the consequences," she adds, ruthlessly.

I grimace. That's fair. My kind of daring should never involve anything that requires balance. "You're right," I say. I go back into the room and grab the notepad that's on the nightstand, and a pen. Mom doesn't object when I tell her I have to hang up because she understands the momentum of the moment.

I sit down on the balcony chair and start a list of what I want —what I actually want, not what Sophie and Nora, or my friends back in Denver, tell me I should want. It's not merely a list of what I *can* have. It starts with "never parallel parking again" and ends with "someone like Hunter" and in between, a life starts to take shape that I didn't expect.

Hunter might not want to hang out that evening for our planned axe-throwing date, but I'm pretty sure he won't ghost me. He's not that kind of guy.

So I'm not surprised when he arrives, shoulders hunched and hands tucked in his jeans pockets, and says, "I'm not sure I'm in the mood for this today."

"I'm so sorry about earlier," I blurt. "I wasn't thinking. I was trying to impress my friends by being...what you called me. Daring."

He stares at me for a moment, and I get smaller under his

gaze. "That's not daring, that's…" he trails off, and I know what he was thinking: stupid. I've been thinking it myself, all day. I've been a woman who can't see herself clearly. If nothing else, this has opened my eyes. Like cleaning a mirror.

"I know." I nod. "I know. Daring is trying something when you're scared, not throwing yourself at a situation to see what happens. You can be daring and plan. You can be daring and careful. I get that. I swear I do."

"I'm really just so mad at Scott for taking you guys out there," Hunter goes on, taking his hands out of his pockets. "He's actually a really good guide. And then he doesn't *think* sometimes."

"He was probably trying to impress Nora. It's a vicious cycle."

Hunter sighs deeply. "It's not…that's not what I want." He swallows, looking down as he fiddles with his hands. "Nora and Scott, revving each other up with their dares and the flirty teasing and counting down until the end."

"That's not what I want either!" Everything feels wrong, like the peace between us has shattered.

He looks up and our eyes connect. The question hangs there between us, unsaid: *Well, what do you want?*

And even though I spent all afternoon trying to figure it out, I'm scared to share my answers. It's too much, too big to spill here, standing in front of a cage in this noisy room full of tipsy people holding sharp objects.

"Maybe we should back off a little," Hunter says, and my heart clenches. "I don't want you to…get hurt."

I wonder if I'm the only one in danger here; I can't tell from the way he looks at me so kindly.

"I'm not going to get hurt," I reply, a hopeful lie.

"It's still a vacation fling," he says. "Even if it doesn't last all vacation."

I'm silent because my throat stops working. I pull in a deep breath through my nose, trying to calm my pounding heart.

Vacation fling. I know that's what it *was,* but I want so much more. I want things I don't quite have words to express yet.

I want to overthrow my whole life for this man and what he represents to me.

It's silly. I would be so silly to say something like that, now, in the face of Hunter naming and dismissing what's between us. He's talking me off a ledge, perhaps. If I can't be daring, I should be grateful.

"Right," I say. "It still could. I'm fine. We're fine." If I keep repeating it, maybe it'll be true.

"So you think...we should keep going? Until the end of the week?"

"Well, why not?" I make my voice flippant. "Do you not want to be with me because of...what happened?"

He shakes his head. "No, that's not it. I'm worried you're doing things only because I want you to."

Shaking my head, I tell him, "*I* want this." My voice is more fierce than I intended.

He nods, like that's settled. "Do you still want an axe-throwing lesson?"

Even as desperately as I want Hunter's nearness, I'm worried the night will end in tears, so I shake my head. "Maybe tomorrow?"

He nods and pats my arm, and we part like that—mostly mutely. I suspect both of us have more to say, yet whatever connection was forming between us was so new, it couldn't withstand a day like this. We broke it. Well, I broke it. By trying so hard at something I shouldn't have said "yes" to.

I wanted to bring a fully-formed plan to this conversation and throw caution to the wind when I presented it. I wasn't ready. And maybe I'll never be ready. Maybe I'm fooling myself.

Walking back to the hotel room—which will be empty, with Sophie and Nora out with Scott and the others again—I pass by a storefront with a little sign that says "attorney at law." I pause and look at it, in the dark window, and I wonder what it's like to work in a town like this. Where the streets are busy but full of people you know. Where the mountains loom not two hours away but minutes. Where you can't find everything you want, but you're more thankful for what's available.

Come back to this if you're brave enough. I make a mental note to myself and I keep walking. Before I get back to the hotel, I get a text from Sophie inviting me to join them at the bar. Well, demanding. I happen to be walking by the bar they're at, so I go in.

They're with Scott at a table in the back, and I can tell as I approach that I'm not going to like what they're talking about, heads bowed over the table and looking serious.

"Hunter's an intense guy," Scott is saying. "He brings his work into everything." He looks up and sees me, standing frozen by the table. "Hey! Let me get you a drink! Beer?" He gets up and while he's gone, Sophie raises her eyebrows meaningfully at Nora.

"I know," Nora says, shaking her head.

"What?" I demand.

"Wrong kind of guy to have a vacation fling with," Sophie says. "Intense? Wants to keep you *safe* from things?"

"Maybe you should cool it with him," Nora suggests.

"Wanting to keep me safe is not a red flag."

"No, but it's something a boyfriend does, not a one-week-stand." Nora makes a face. "We shouldn't have encouraged you to get involved with him. He's kind of serious. That's not the plan."

"Yeah," Sophie agrees. "He's too much for you. We leave in a few days. You need someone to get you out of your head and leave you refreshed, not a complication that's going to confuse you."

"We don't want this to drag out," Nora adds. "You're bored, not…you know, one of those Hallmark heroines looking for a small town guy to run away with."

And for once, instead of thinking to myself that my friends might be right, deep in my gut I reject what they're saying. Because I know myself better. I know what I'm looking for and maybe it's not Hallmark, but it's not a refreshing *fling*, either.

Scott comes back with drinks and they turn from the subject. I take a beer and nurse it slowly while I think about what they said.

I can't help it: I hope they're right about Hunter. Because they might be wrong about what I'm looking for in my life.

The next morning, instead of going on a horseback ride with the group, I go back to the lawyer's office. Because I *am* daring, damnit, and more importantly, now I know the difference between wisely daring and stupidly daring.

The attorney's name is Roger Smith and he's ancient. I watch him get up and slowly walk to the door through the glass. It takes several minutes. I listen to the sound of birds and tourists passing as I wait. It's nice. It's peaceful.

"Hello there," he says once he finally makes it to the door. "How can I help you?"

This is not going to be easy. I don't know what I expected—him to take one look at me and ask if I wanted a job? I force myself to dive in. "Hello, my name is Mollie. I'm a paralegal in Denver. I wondered if I could ask you a few questions about working in law in a small town?"

"Hm," he says, and studies me.

It seems one thing attorneys in big cities and small towns

have in common is they don't like someone wasting billable time. Amid the risk I'm taking, that gives me some comfort.

"The practice is about the same. Different scenery. Slower, perhaps."

I nod quickly, bobbing my head like a doll. "That makes sense." My feet want to run away from this awkward conversation. "I'm just...looking to make a change. I'm tired of, well, of the scenery."

He opens the door a little further for me. I guess he's decided I'm worth his time. "Work is work, no matter where it is. You don't like what you do in the city, you're not going to like it anywhere else."

Considering this, I bite my lip. "I like my work. It's my life I don't like in the city." I say it like a confession, like he's a priest who's going to provide me some way to cleanse myself of the sin of being unhappy. I gather myself and straighten my spine so that I can ask for what I really want. "I wondered if you knew of any small town attorneys who might need a paralegal?"

He surveys me through rheumy eyes for another long moment, the sound of the street and my nervous heart all I can hear. At the last minute, I couldn't voice exactly what I wanted, but it turns out this man is kind enough to hear what I can't say.

"Why not here?" he asks, and lets me in.

HUNTER

THIS IS what I agreed to, after all. A vacation fling with someone I don't know that well and never will.

By the time I meet Mollie for another axe-throwing lesson, I've convinced myself nothing's changed. We were never meant to last longer than a week, and anything more was all in my head.

So I try not to be weird with her. And it mostly works—coaching her through bad habits she's somehow already formed is distracting—except she keeps asking me if I'm OK.

"Nora said you and Scott aren't talking."

"We're not *not* talking." When we tried to talk about it, Scott said something like "I shouldn't have encouraged her into a situation she wasn't comfortable with" and I felt the situation never should have been an option in the first place. So now I'm not sure I can trust him on outings, and that means I'm doing extra work to make up for his poor judgment. Tom doesn't seem to notice, and if I said something, I'm not sure which way it would go—

Scott fired or me dressed down? Neither result is something I'm comfortable with. So not talking is the best choice right now.

"It's not his fault," Mollie offers.

"It's pretty much completely his fault," I counter.

"Well, Nora did ask him to take us on the craziest hike he's ever done near town."

Of course she did. I scowl and shake my head. "He's the professional. He should have known better."

"He was off duty."

I'm not sure why we're arguing about this. It's making the back of my neck hot. "I don't want to talk about it anymore," I say, and we fall into a silence that's similar to the one between me and Scott.

Mollie's not getting any better at axe-throwing. I keep correcting her form and explaining follow-through and timing on her throws and most of the time, she can hit the target. She's not *accurate.* In the tournament we have scheduled tomorrow to celebrate the end of the week's tour, she'll get knocked out right away despite all the practice.

And my frustration makes me a terrible coach. She's not *getting* it—just like she doesn't get that what I really want is a quiet moment where I can tuck her safely under my arm and feel safe. She can't land the axe and she can't make me feel like everything's OK because we're not.

Inviting her back to my place is out, because Tom's likely there. The last thing I need is to exacerbate the tension between us. I haven't been into his office since our last conversation.

And yet I need to touch Mollie like I need water. And our time is so short now. At the end of the lesson, I explain that the house is busy tonight and add, "I still owe you that massage."

"Do you want to go back to my hotel room? Nora and Sophie are out with the other guys." Mollie smiles back at me tentatively, graciously accepting my attempt to backtrack to where we'd been a day ago. "Maybe you can give me some tips and I can return the favor."

We walk back to her hotel, me carrying the bag of custom axes I brought with me to throw. They didn't help Mollie's aim much. Maybe she needs a different weight on hers. We could look into an axe customized to her. Well, if we had more time and she wasn't leaving soon. I keep thinking of things we could do in the future and reminding myself we don't have that.

"Scott told Nora and Sophie you're intense and now they think you're wrong for me." Mollie says it in a rush, like she's been thinking about it all night. We're almost back to the hotel when it comes out.

"Intense," I repeat, for now ignoring the fact I've lost her friends' favor. It's kind of a relief, actually. Maybe they won't be constantly talking about me behind my back. "Actually," I say as I'm realizing it. "Wait, are your friends badmouthing me now? They thanked me for saving you on that pipe!"

"No, no," Mollie says quickly. "I mean, they just think you're...you know...boyfriend material."

Stopping still on the sidewalk, I stare at Mollie. *Boyfriend material.* And that's a bad thing? "That's the first time anyone's called me boyfriend material. Most people would say I have no future, no prospects, and no benefits. I thought that's what your friends liked about me, actually. I'm...*easy.*"

Mollie winces. "You're not easy. Not like that."

"Well, I'm not Scott," I say bitterly. "Pretty sure he never even thinks about the future."

"That's the problem," she says. "Now that they know you think about the future, they're worried that..." She cuts herself off.

"I might think about a future with you," I finish, my voice soaked in the knowledge that I do exactly that. "And they don't want that for you."

"Well that's what *they* think…"

"It's fine," I say quickly. "We clearly *don't* have a future. They don't have anything to worry about."

"But." She clearly struggles to come up with what comes after a "but" here, and I let her. "Why?" she finally asks.

I'm not sure why she's dragging this out. It's painful. *You wouldn't keep hiking through a blister, Hunter*—that's what Tom would say, and ask why I kept going in this conversation. Still, I can't walk away from Mollie, even though it hurts to stay. She doesn't deserve that. "You don't even live here," I finally offer in response.

"But if I did…"

"Even if you did, we're not exactly compatible. I mean, I live outdoors and you work in an office. This stuff is my life and for you it's a vacation."

"And I'm bad at it." Her shoulders slump in a way I hate.

"I didn't say that."

She shrugs. "It's OK. It's true." She bites her lip. "So even if some things changed, this still wouldn't be…it's not something you want for the future?"

I know a test question when I hear one. And we promised each other this wasn't more. I know Mollie now. I know she pushes through what she doesn't want in order to live up to other people's expectations. I don't want to be just another person whose expectations she's trying to live up to. Without hesitating, I firmly shake my head. "No."

Her smile up at me is a little watery. "Then I guess we better enjoy what we have while we can. You know, one week only."

"Is that what you *really* want?" I study her closely. I'm a guide. Not only do I need to be aware of my own pain points, I need to know the people I'm leading aren't hiding things from me that could become big problems farther down the trail.

And maybe I'm wrong. Maybe Mollie does want me. But I

have to hear her say it. I'm not going to push her into an adventure she doesn't want to have.

"This week has been sort of life-changing," Mollie says. "I mean, I had a life-or-death experience and I've tried things I never thought I would try. And being with you the other night was so different from what I expected. All of it has made me, I don't know, more alive. I haven't felt like that in a long time. So if you don't mind, yeah, I still want to be with you. While I can."

While I can. That was the last thing I wanted to hear. And yet for the same reasons Mollie articulated—she makes me feel more than I have in a long time—I can't say no. "OK. Maybe we'll make an axe-throwing professional out of you yet, then."

She smiles. "Let's start with that massage."

So we do. Naked massage, because why wouldn't we? Back in Mollie's hotel room, I run my fingers up and down her bare back, stunned by the softness of her skin against my calluses.

She shivers beneath me, and I apologize for the roughness of my hands.

"I like it," she says, the kind of thing I bet Scott hears every night. Not me. To me, these words are precious acceptance. Mollie knows what I am and what I do—and why all of that means we can't be together—and chooses to be with me like this anyway. Of course it's temporary, but temporary is extraordinary.

And Mollie is extraordinary, her body shaping itself to my hands. The curves around her hips and butt are the perfect diameter, my fingers making dents in her flesh as though marking they were there. My dick hardens against her back, ready to find its way inside her again. Not yet, though. First, I sweep my hands over her back, under her breasts, and back up her neck through her hair. I'm not really massaging, I'm feeling my way. Remembering my map.

She turns over and stretches out beneath me, and I fit

between her thighs perfectly. My hair cascades around us, curtaining my face and hers like we're in our own private world. I meet her eyes and wonder if, in an alternate reality or parallel universe, we could be together. Perhaps a world where I'm less judgy and she's less afraid of what people think. Or a world where none of that matters because we live in the same town.

I enter her, meeting no resistance. It could be the first time, or the thousandth, and I will always be able to find my way back here. Someday, years from now, I will wake up remembering the way I slid into her channel, my hands wrapped around her hips, my tongue tickling her nipple, and felt like I'd found the best trail in the world. The kind of hike men like me dream about—the secret ones, that lead to something extraordinary, something no one can simply tell you about, something you have to experience for yourself and guard closely like a secret only to be shared with the most extraordinary people you know. The people you want to hold as closely as you do your secret trails.

"To be clear, this isn't how I would massage most people," I tell her.

She laughs. "I bet you tell that to all the girls."

She's joking, we both are, but my objection clogs my throat for a moment. *There are no other girls.*

Surely there will be in the future, though. Some perfect woman who wants to live where I live and do what I do and tries really hard at everything she does and has short hair and laughs when I touch her with my callused hands?

Opening my mouth, I'm not sure what to say but I know I need to say something. Deny that I don't want this. Admit that she's the only woman who's ever made me want to break the rules. Tell her she's the secret trail I've searched for my whole life.

Then we hear the sound of the hotel door's key lock. I roll off, landing on the floor, and Mollie and I both grab at bedding to cover our nakedness.

"Oh my god!" Sophie shouts. "What are you doing on my bed?"

Nora follows her in and surveys us coolly, me barely covering my balls with an edge of the duvet. "Those comforters never get washed, you know."

"And now we *see* what people do with them!" Sophie adds. "Oh my god, it smells like sex in here. Open a window or something!"

"Um, could you turn around or something while I grab my pants?" I'm trying to be reasonable, but this is embarrassing. Heat climbs the back of my neck. Mollie, clutching a pillow to her chest, looks back at me with wide eyes.

"I'm sorry," she mouths, then glowers at her friends. "You guys weren't supposed to be back yet."

"Well, *somebody* got so drunk they weren't going to be much use to me," Nora says. She glares at Hunter. "I think you're making him depressed."

"Scott?" I blink back at her, momentarily forgetting the chill around my dick. Only momentarily. "Wait. Can we have this conversation when I'm fully clothed please?"

Nora and Sophie both roll their eyes and make a show out of turning their backs. I grab my clothes and put them on as fast as I do when I'm camping in freezing weather and just crawled out of my sleeping bag. My dick has shriveled from its previous enthusiastic state. When I look over, Mollie only has her bra and a pair of shorts on.

"We're decent," she says, and pulls a t-shirt over her head. Her friends turn around, arms folded over both chests.

"Hunter, you can leave," Nora says. "Maybe go check on Scott."

"Yeah, we made sure he got home OK but he was a mess," Sophie adds.

Mollie nods at me. Reluctant to abandon her when her friends look so serious, I stubbornly kiss her on the cheek beneath their judgy gazes before I go. "I'll see you tomorrow," I say. "Text me if..." I trail off, because I'm not sure how to finish that. Mollie doesn't need me. We made sure of that with our deal.

"Last day to become an expert outdoorswoman!"

From her eyes, I can tell that she's pretending to be cheerful, and I pause before I grab my jacket and shoes off the floor. She smiles and Nora clears her throat, so I guess this isn't the moment to follow up.

As the hotel door closes behind me, I hear Nora saying to Mollie, "Is this an addiction? Do you need an intervention?"

I walk away—practice for the real thing—and like I will be later this week, I'm sure I'm doing the wrong thing. I'm not going to check on Scott; I'm going to hold tightly to the comforting fact that he and Mollie proved we're all wrong together. I'm going to hold tightly to the very real fact that this week will end, she will go home, and I will never forget the moment I almost asked her not to go. And didn't.

sixteen

MOLLIE

STRANGELY, I'm not that nervous about the axe-throwing tournament. Maybe it's a false sense of confidence from all my practicing? False because even in practice, I'm not very good.

Hunter is sure that, if I keep at it, everything will click into place. "You're wearing a new groove," he says. Maybe if I trust the process hard enough, he'll start to believe the same thing about us, too. We just need to click in place.

Maybe today is the day everything starts working.

So I'm hopeful, walking into the alley wearing my lucky red shoes. I'm dressed in one of the many "date" outfits I brought on this trip and have not needed because we've mostly done athletic activities. I think I look cuter than I normally do when Hunter sees me, and I'm excited to get his reaction.

Instead of looking shocked—underneath all that dirt is a pretty girl?—he smiles at me normally and gives my hand a little squeeze. "You OK?" he asks.

My nod is probably too quick for someone in the middle of a life transition. I think he's talking about Nora and Sophie and last night, and that's all fine. Other than being blocked from having more great sex, or the conversation Hunter and I really needed to have.

My friends won't stop bugging me about how I've "gone local" or whatever, like this town and Hunter have sucked me into some kind of parallel universe without my own volition. I can handle my friends' concerns. We'll soon be separated by time and geography and they will forget to worry about me.

Most of the other people from the tour are here, even the younger guys I've tried to avoid on every outing. They're mostly keeping to themselves tonight, so maybe they finally got the message I'm not interested. Tyler and Zoe came to the tournament, along with Tom. There's no Scott. I'm worried about the way Hunter is holding my dumb decision against his friend. He shuts me out when I bring it up, and there's no way to ask about it privately in front of all the people readying for the tournament.

For now, I'm annoyed that Nora and Sophie are somehow better at axe-throwing than me. Me, the person who's invested actual time in learning!

Well, Nora used to play baseball and Sophie grew up playing soccer, so those things might have helped them build the muscle memory Hunter's always talking about.

I try to comfort myself with logic as I watch them throw and hit the target every time.

We're playing a round robin bracket, so even when I'm terrible, I don't get knocked out. It was Hunter's idea and I wonder if it was for my sake.

By the second round of matches, it's obvious that I'm in last place. By a lot.

"You don't have to keep throwing," Sophie tells me. "We'd all understand." Her sympathy makes me want to prove that I *can* do this. If I keep *trying*, surely I'll get a different result.

"No, want to," I insist. I've had more beer than I intended due to self-pity and I'm a little woozy when I stand to take my turn. I grab the table.

"Seriously, Mollie," Nora says. "Why don't you sit this one out."

I glare at her. "I can *do* it. I've been practicing."

"You're only doing it for *him*," Nora hisses, like everyone's not standing right there, close enough to hear even a low comment.

I'm afraid to look, but out of the corner of my eye, I sense Hunter jerk away. Like he doesn't want to be involved in this at all.

"That's not true," I say, my eyes prickling. *Oh no.* I can't drunk cry right now. Not because nothing is going the way I want, despite my best efforts. Not because Hunter thinks I only do things because other people want me to. It's not true. It can't be.

"You'd never even thought of axe throwing before and now you're like a groupie," Nora replies. She glances around at everyone looking and looks a little regretful. "Sorry, it's true. This isn't you. It's him."

Hunter walks away. He leaves the group, grabs his jacket, and exits the venue.

"Nora!" I grit out. "You're the one who wanted me to *find my thing* this week. And now you're angry I'm doing something you wouldn't do?"

"I wanted you to find yourself, not find a bandwagon to hop onto," Nora says stubbornly.

Sophie puts her hand on our friend's shoulder. "Nora..."

The rest of the group is dispersing, finding this heated argument more awkward than expected. Someone grabs the empty beer pitchers and walks away with them. A few people go back to axe-throwing. I hope someone went after Hunter.

Nora isn't done. "Do you even like him or are you just unhappy?"

Glaring at her so hard a twinge of a headache starts behind my eyes, I bite my tongue. Because I know she's wrong, and I can't articulate why. Sure, Hunter prompted my self-reflection. And he's on my list of things I want. But there's a lot more on it. Things that connect, that form a vague outline of the life I want. I can't see it clearly yet. I'm trying. I'm trying so hard and I'm worried no matter how much effort I put in, it will be like axe-throwing and I'll never get what I want.

"I *am* unhappy," I say, and start to cry. "Why are you trying to take some happiness away from me?"

"Oh..." Nora and Sophie both surround me, hugging me tightly in a friend sandwich.

"We don't want you to make decisions while you're unhappy that mess up the rest of your life," Sophie says softly.

"I'm trying to make the rest of my life better," I sniffle. "It's not about *him*. It's about me."

"OK, boo," Nora says, resting her chin on the top of my much shorter head. "I'm sorry. I should have listened more instead of going off like that."

They let me sniffle softly for a few more minutes, and then Nora—being Nora—can't help herself. She makes her point.

"You should still break up with him and come home," she adds. "I'm not wrong about that. You need some distance."

I wipe my nose on her shirt in response.

"Give her a minute, Nora," Sophie hisses.

"I'm going to listen to my own voice, you guys," I say quietly. "The two of you can't decide things for me."

Clearing my throat, I straighten my shoulders. That voice is still quiet, but I'm starting to be able to hear it better. And I'm determined to let it get loud.

* * *

Dorothy knows me now when I come into the coffee shop. It's one of my proudest accomplishments on this trip. I had no idea how satisfying it was to be known by the people around me, not just be another face in the crowd or woman catcalled on the street.

Taking my order to the table by the front window, I sit down and wait. I was early, but Hunter arrives not long after me. Long and lanky, he slides into the chair across from me, then hops back up to order a muffin.

I'm nervous. I know what I need to say, and I'm also worried emotions will get in the way. So I dive in before asking him how he is or what he's thinking. "So, I've decided to move," I squeak out.

He raises his eyebrows. "Where?"

"Here." I clear my throat when he blinks back at me. "I am going to work with Mr. Smith."

"Mr. Rogers?"

"What? No, Roger Smith."

"Sorry. Right. People in town call him Mr. Rogers because of the sweaters. Never mind." Hunter seems nervous, too. Not in the happy, excited way I'd hoped for. "Don't you have a job?"

That's a bad sign. Does he *want* me to leave? "I have a job I hate. In a city I hate. I like it here."

He licks his lips. "This isn't because..." His brow bunches. He runs a hand through his hair and strands of it come loose from his bun. "Because of me?"

I know what he wants me to say. "No!" But it's also true. The way this town has welcomed me—from the blueberry and lemon curd muffins Dorothy now always has ready for me to the lawyers who open their doors for no reason—means as much to me as Hunter calling me *sweet and spicy*. I can be the me I want to be here.

"It doesn't have to be a thing," I insist. "We can just be people who, you know, say hello in the coffee shop." That wasn't what I intended to say when I arrived at this coffee shop, after practicing my "what if we try?" speech. With the worried expression on Hunter's face, how can I not reassure him?

"OK..." He frowns and looks out the window at the people passing on the street. "Are you sure about this? I mean, it's not always the easiest place to live. The winters are long and it's expensive."

Even though I told myself I didn't expect his reaction to be "now we can be together, yey," I'm still gutted by his lack of enthusiasm. Doesn't he want me here, at least a little bit?

The lump of tears goes down hard when I swallow. "Yes, I mean. I want to try it." Then I can't think of anything else to say after that.

"Well, you are the best at trying things," he says, with a little smile that I try to take as encouragement. We both look at the table for an excruciating beat of silence. I force myself to take a drink of my latte.

"Right. So. I wanted you to know," I say finally.

"I hope you'll keep up your axe-throwing and mountain biking while you're here."

"That's the hope!" My voice is overly perky, but I can't help it. This conversation is like drowning. I'm so excited about my new plans, and they suddenly feel so lonely without even the assurance of one friend in this town.

"Well, I'll be around. If you need to practice." He nods to himself and eats the last of his muffin. I know what he thinks. He thinks I'm latching onto him like a stalker. That's more or less the impression Nora and Sophie gave him. And I can't let him think that. I can't let that be the reality.

OK, I need to let him go. Hunter doesn't owe me anything. He expected this to be a one-week fling. Now he has to be nice and tip his hat to me when he sees me around town. "That'd be great, but no pressure," I offer. *I'll die a little inside every time I see you and can't touch you. Every time my mental map of your body fades a little bit more.*

We smile at each other politely for a few more moments before Hunter stands. I watch him throw his wrapper and napkin away, unable to move from the table. Then he says, "I'll see you around, Mollie. Let me know if you need anything." And he leaves.

I'm staring blankly at my empty latte mug when Dorothy comes up to the table and sets down a croissant. "On the house, honey," she says. "You look like you could use something sweet."

"Thanks," I whisper.

"Of course." She places her palm on my shoulder and squeezes. "You're one of us and we take care of our own, here. Welcome home."

* * *

Nora and Sophie called my mother. Now they're packing to leave while my mom is on her way here, and they're satisfied they "did the right thing" and aren't leaving me "to my own devices."

They still think I'm only doing this for Hunter. I tried to explain that Hunter and I aren't going to last past the week, and Sophie shook her head. "That's what you say, but it's not what you *think*."

She's wrong. I saw how differently Hunter looked at me after the incident on the water pipe. Scott did too, and apologized to me last night for "putting you in danger and messing up your thing with Hunter."

Of course I forgave him. He wasn't the only person involved. I think Hunter maybe left open the possibility of a future before that, and now he doesn't, and it's my fault. I confused daring with a bad decision. And now he probably thinks that's what I'm doing by moving.

We all went out for most people's last night in Telluride. Almost everyone came to the bar except Hunter. I kept watching the door for him, hoping he would show up for at least a few minutes, and he never did. Tom said something about him being home with his head between a book's cover.

I have goals beyond Hunter. I practice listing them in my head the day between Sophie and Nora's departure and my mom's arrival. My mom will blow in like a hurricane, with force. Before she gets here, I spend the day walking the streets of my new home and looking at apartments. Everything is *expensive*—worse than Denver. The niggling doubts I've successfully hidden so far start to sound louder.

Maybe this *is* foolish. Uprooting my life for a man is one thing, but uprooting it for the sense of peace I find in a certain place? Maybe I can find or create that somehow back where I currently live—even though so far I've been unable. Maybe I need to try harder.

Still, Hunter proves that trying doesn't always win.

When Mom gets there, she doesn't address the reason she came flying across the country right away. Instead, she sits across from me at Dorothy's cafe and critiques the town newspaper. "Look at this," she says, her finger darting between headlines. "All of these headlines are from wire services. This one doesn't even have anything to do with Telluride. This could be better." She fans through the pages, saying "hm" every once in a while.

"This is cute," she adds, showing me a column with a woman's face in a box on top. "Paula. A local perspective. Apparently short term housing is a big issue here." She keeps paging through the issue.

"It isn't bad, in the end," she finally says. "So few towns even have local news anymore. Clearly ad-supported; look at the pages and pages of them. They must have enough money to fix some of these problems. Hm. Interesting. There are only two people on the masthead as staff."

Watching her puzzle through the business model, I smiled a little to myself. My mom, who had me later in life, has been talking about retirement for a few years now. She's so immersed in her industry and her career that I worry she'll die at her desk. But analyzing this newspaper has brought her to life in a way I haven't seen in awhile.

"So," she says, putting the paper down and focusing that analysis on me. "Your friends tell me you've gone crazy."

"I'm not *crazy*," I protest. "Just because I want to move here."

"Nothing wrong with going a little crazy once in a while. It's how most people get big things done." My mom takes a sip of her latte and then gives it a second look. "Mm. The question is whether this is a big thing or you running away."

Unfortunately, I'm not sure of the answer myself. I stare back at my mother. "Let me show you around town," I suggest. "Maybe you'll understand why I like it."

She nods slowly, and I can tell she has more questions. "And the boy?" She raises an eyebrow at me. "What's going on with that?"

"That's...not going anywhere. We were a vacation fling. Moving here doesn't change that."

"In a town this size, you'll see him constantly. How are you going to handle that?"

Biting my lip, I consider this. It's a fair question, and one that's been haunting me. Zoe mentioned that the dating pool here is pretty small, too. "Well...I don't want to have one of those situations that drags on or is on-and-off-again because we're bored and in the same place. Either we're together or we're not. And we're not. So I can be friendly but that doesn't mean I'm going to pine for him." I think of Zoe and Tyler as I say this, even though I'm not sure that's their relationship. They rarely hold hands or show affection in public. Yet they seem to date exclusively despite their casual attitudes.

Mom gives a decisive nod. "There's no need for pining. You can get on with your life without a man holding you back." That's what she's always done, so I guess I have a good example. "But—that's not why you want to move?"

"It's not!" I insist. "I love it here. You'll see. It's so much better than the city, where you don't know anyone and you have to parallel park all the time."

She snorts. "Where there's museums and theatre and shopping malls?"

"Mother. When is the last time you went to the theatre." I say the word with drama, like I have an accent.

She smiles, like she knows something I don't. "I went on a date the other week to the theatre, you little whippersnapper."

"You were on a *date*?"

"I'm 65, not dead."

Setting aside that startling news—the idea I could gain a step-father at this point in my life had never occurred to me—I go back to convincing my mother Telluride is a great place to live.

She meets Dorothy, and the two of them discuss the recipe for Victorian sponge cake. Apparently my mother is guilty of overbeating every time she bakes. Dorothy gets to the heart of the matter immediately: "Do you have too much stress in your life?"

My mom gives me a look when I can't help a snort. "Some would say that," she admits.

Then we walk down the street to the bridge over the creek and look up at the mountains. It's hot, with a cool breeze blowing down on us. "Well, I don't think you could pick a *prettier* place," Mom acknowledges.

We look at a few apartments, all of them in shared houses charging high rent. She's not impressed. "Do you really want to live with strangers?" she asks.

"Well, no," I admit. "But I want to live here and it's been hard to find something reasonable."

When we walk back through town, we come across Tyler and Zoe and she startles. I don't watch football and I never looked Tyler up, but Nora and Sophie told me he used to be a big deal. "Is that…"

"Don't make a big deal out of it," I murmur, cutting off my mom before she brow-beats Tyler into a spontaneous interview for her paper. "He hates that."

Her journalism spidey-senses are clearly pinging, although she doesn't say anything when I introduce the couple by their first names. "Zoe writes for the paper you were looking at," I add, to distract her. "My mom runs a newspaper back in the city," I explain.

"I'm sure it's a bigger production than this one," Zoe says with a smile. "Although the actual production of this newspaper is a pretty big deal. Mark has to drive over an hour to get print copies."

My mom starts grilling Zoe on what she covers, so I step to the side with Tyler. I want to ask him if he's seen Hunter, but that would be silly. Hunter isn't going to confide in Tyler, even— or especially—if he had something to confide such as, "I miss Mollie."

So I ask him where in town he thinks I should take my mom for dinner, instead.

Later, still wandering around town as the sun sets and we have to put on jackets, we even run into Mr. Rogers—Roger

Smith, that is, my soon-to-be-boss—wearing a signature button-up sweater.

"It's too much work for me," he admits to my mom, when she bluntly asks why he wants to hire me. "I'm supposed to be retired! And here I am, notarizing documents and filing all my own busywork."

"Are you? Retired?" My mom looks keenly interested. I wonder if she's actually thinking about this for herself, or if she's formulating a story about life after retirement for the newspaper.

"Well, I retired from my practice in the city, moved here, and got bored! I didn't want to sit around on my porch all day, not using my brain anymore," he says. "Turns out, there's plenty of work to be had here. Administrative stuff, you know. I still make people drive to Montrose or Grand Junction for the big things and specialty work. It's a slower pace than my heyday, but that's about right for me now."

Over dinner, we sit at the bar and my mom talks to the people next to us about ski season here. She loves to ski but the drive from Denver to the mountains on winter weekends has become prohibitive.

By this point, my mom has talked to almost more people in Telluride than I have. She must be formulating an essay on the town in her mind. It will be complete with pros *and* cons, I have no doubt.

When we get back to our hotel room—the same one Nora and Sophie vacated the other day—my mom surprises me. She turns to me and says, "I like it here. I think I should move here myself." Her eyes twinkling, she unlocks the door and walks in.

Blinking in her wake, I wonder if my mom is unhappy too. Or if I'm not quite as crazy as I've been led to believe.

seventeen

HUNTER

IT'S BEEN RAINING every afternoon of this backpacking trip, so we have a lot of down time. We don't force the miles when it will be a slog for the hikers. At least this group hasn't complained as much as some of them do.

For the first two days, I avoid Scott. It's easy enough; he doesn't go out of his way to talk to me, either. There's a woman on the trip who is exactly Scott's type: pretty and jokes about everything, including the mud. He spends most of his time flirting with Diana.

Not that he isn't meeting the requirements of his job. He's meticulous about it. When he leads, he explains the route and shows the map to the group. When he brings up the rear, he counts the hikers and checks with the slow ones on hot spots in their shoes and cramps in their legs. He does it all quietly, only laughing and joking when we're all seated around the campfire at night or huddled under dripping trees in the middle of the day. Keeping everyone's spirits up. Just another part of his job.

And there's no reason for me to doubt him, not really. I

know Scott's good at his job, and I'm reminded of it daily as I watch him closely for mistakes. He catches me watching him and says nothing, simply carrying on like nothing is off. I wouldn't blame him for getting angry, not really. I'm not Scott's boss. I don't have any business judging his work. Still, he simply lets me watch. And keeps proving himself, damn him.

By the third day, the hikers have questions. A trip like this tends to bond people quickly, all of us out in the woods with nothing but each other to lean on. They're looking for distraction from the discomfort of heavy bags and tired feet.

It starts with Scott's current love interest. "Are you two in the middle of some kind of bro fight?" Diana when we're all waiting out another rain storm. Scott and I are stationed at either end of the group, not looking at each other.

"Yeah, you never talk to each other." Another hiker chimes in —Sara, a mom who came on this trip without her kids and has made everyone around her a stand-in.

"We've done this trip so many times, we don't really need to confer anymore," I offer, refusing to look down at Scott.

"You go out of your way not to," someone else says. People become more observant on these trips, too. It starts out with a lot of questions about the flowers and the trees and turns into questions about life and relationships. I should have remembered that. It's one reason why Scott hooks up with someone on or after almost every trip: the false closeness and the close encounter with existence.

"He's mad at me," Scott volunteers then, inflaming my annoyance with him. "I did something stupid and he hasn't forgiven me."

I grit my teeth to avoid snapping that he doesn't *deserve* forgiveness. Not yet.

"What kind of stupid?" The group is intrigued now.

"Yeah, like, sleep with his wife stupid or ate his leftovers stupid?"

"Unsafe stupid," I grumble under my breath. Might not be the smartest thing to let this group know their guide—who they trust to get them home again—makes unsafe decisions. I am still seething with anger over what Scott did, taking Mollie into a situation like that. Sure, he might seem good at his job, but I can't let my guard down. Someone could have gotten hurt.

"What was that?" Without looking, I sense the entire group leaning my direction.

"I took his girlfriend on a hike she wasn't ready for," Scott says. He's speaking calmly, like he's given this a lot of thought. "And I shouldn't have. It was stupid and I'm sorry. I'm sorry I took anyone on that hike, and especially her."

"She's not my girlfriend," I say, which wasn't what I meant to respond. It comes out anyway.

"I'm sorry about that, too," Scott says quietly.

"*That's* not your fault," I admit. Suddenly, I miss Mollie desperately. She would tell me to forgive Scott. That they both made dumb decisions in the moment.

The group of hikers between us are moving their heads back and forth, ping-ponging attention as we speak over their heads.

"Was it because of the hike though?" asks Diana.

"No, I don't think so," I say, after a brief hesitation. Things changed after. All along, I told myself I knew we would end, and that's what made it real. Mollie was one of those women in town to experiment with adventure and maybe a little recklessness. She wasn't looking for something steady. And that's all I am, really. Steady. I can't help myself. "I was just an adventure to her, nothing more."

"That's bullshit and if you pulled your head out of a book, you'd know that. The only reason she was up there was to impress you," Scott snaps.

"He wasn't even there," says one of the men. He sounds confused.

"She knew he liked that she tried everything," Scott explains. "So she was trying out being a daredevil."

"I don't want to date a daredevil," I snap. I hate the idea that Mollie only does things because I want her to. What happens when she gets tired of them? Then she'll be tired of me, too.

"I know that," Scott says. "And maybe she doesn't know what you want. Because you haven't told her."

Everyone falls silent. The group is looking at me, waiting for me to process this.

"I told her...we were just a vacation fling," I say, swallowing back the bile over this expression. "That's what I want."

"Man, you've never wanted a fling in your life. You commit to everything you do."

Except her. The words are silent, and he might as well have said them for how loud they are in my mind.

"She was leaving," I finally say. "She was going back to the city."

"Was?" Sara—such a mom—picks up on this immediately.

"She told me she'd decided to stay. Before we left on this trip," I admit. It's all I've been thinking about. Mollie staying. I half expect, when we get back to town, to find that she changed her mind and left after all. That she was only staying for me, and I took that approval away from her.

"Why?" Diana asks the obvious question. "Because of you?"

"No," I say slowly. "She said even though we weren't together, she still wanted to move here."

"She's like you," Scott says. "She commits."

"We were only going to last a week. We were never *together*."

"Sometimes a vacation fling turns into more," says Diana. He shifts uncomfortably. They'll likely be having a conversation later. Scott's flings never turn into *more*.

"We *committed* to that, though," I say, using Scott's word. "To just a vacation...thing." I hate the other word so I don't use it.

"Maybe you hold too tightly to your commitments sometimes," Sara suggests. "Maybe it gives you blind spots."

"When you're on a bike, it makes sense to stick to your line, but if you're climbing and refuse to adjust your planned route when you see a better hold, you fall," Scott says. He sounds like Tom in that moment with his athletic metaphors.

Tom, somebody who refuses to see me as more than a guide. When I *know* I can be more.

Maybe I did the same thing to Mollie. Maybe I didn't see more. And maybe I can only see Scott one way, too.

"When you took her on that hike," I say slowly. "Did you have more than one route in mind?"

"Of course," Scott says. "I wasn't going to make them do anything. It was their choice."

"And you think Mollie only did that to impress me?"

"She says yes to everything when you're involved, man," he says.

"It doesn't seem sustainable," I say, worried. What if she moves and regrets getting carried away?

"Love can surprise you," Sara says. A couple of the men scoff. "No, really," she insists. "People change their lives for less."

"I mean, I wouldn't know," Scott says. "Hunter, though, basically does everything for love. That's why he commits so hard. And I don't know Mollie that well, but I think she might be the same. If she loves it here, who's to tell her that's not a good enough reason to move? That's why I moved here. And it's why you stayed."

"That's true," I acknowledge.

"So why is it OK for you and not for her?"

Diana the obvious question, and I hear it, but I can't say the answer out loud: *Because I have no future and Mollie should.*

Maybe the problem has been me, all along.

"So, are you two going to make up, now?" Sara asks.

"It's OK if you can't forgive me," Scott says. "Yet. I mean, you will eventually, right?"

I frown down at the forest floor beneath me. It's stopped raining, and the sun is already back out. Things are starting to warm up and dry out. Without rain, there's very little moisture in the air here.

Standing up, I walk past the group of curious faces to Scott. He stands up to meet me, and looks like he's bracing himself. Like I might punch him. I've never punched anyone in my life and I'm not going to start now.

"Think twice before you invite someone to do something you would do next time," I say, meeting his eyes for the first time in days. "You're not a good gauge for what people should be doing."

He winces, and I feel the rest of the group react the same way.

"I get it," Scott says. "I make choices that more reasonable people, people who care about the future, shouldn't make. It's fine," he adds to the group.

"That was a little harsh," Diana says.

"Sorry," I say automatically. "Maybe it was."

Scott smiles and claps me on the back. "Maybe you're not a very good gauge for less serious people, Hunter. The rest of us should probably think twice before doing serious things, like you said."

If I'm a serious person, I don't need to mess around with this fake affection bullshit. So I give him a hug. The group of hikers cheers and claps.

Then, working together, Scott and I gather them and their gear and head back down the trail. We have two days left of this trip. I plan to spend it thinking about what I actually want from my future—and how to get it.

eighteen

MOLLIE

MOM BUYS A CONDO—SHE plans to spend a chunk of the winter in town—and I move into it. It takes a month and a few trips back and forth between the city. I sell a lot of my crappy, one-season furniture and discover I don't really own that much that I want to keep. Mom sends a truckload of her nicer things, saying it's a good investment for when she spends time there.

The whole move, I ask myself, "Am I overreacting? Am I being too hasty?" Then I get a ticket for my car edging into the sidewalk while I'm loading boxes into it—I have nowhere else to park!—and my so-called friends bail on helping me pack to go to brunch. I'm ready, if nothing else, for something different. I can always move back to the city if I don't like it in Telluride long-term.

"Life is about change," Mom says. "It's about trying things, seeing if they work out, and then adjusting accordingly. We're doing the same thing right now, you and I. We're trying something new to see how it goes. We can always change our minds."

Hopefully my mom doesn't change her mind before I do, because I really can't afford this move without her.

My—our—new apartment is within walking distance to Main Street in Telluride. I could go to Dorothy's for coffee every morning on my way to work, commuting by foot. I can see the mountains from our little balcony. And there's a sheltered spot to park, so I won't be battling snow in the winter. It's perfect. It's everything I envisioned when I allowed myself to dream.

Zoe, who helped me move in, asks me how I'm going to fill my time outside of work. It's a new concept—the idea that I need a hobby. And I realize that what I really want is to do what Hunter told me to do and keep trying new things. So I join a book club and a painting class. I go axe-throwing with Zoe and Tyler, even though I'm still terrible at it.

I have long conversations with Zoe, who understands the challenges of moving to Telluride. She's a local who moved away and then came back. She didn't move because of Tyler, she tells me, but he helped inspire the move.

"Inspire." That's her word.

"He made me feel OK about the inevitability," she explains. "Change is hard without a little incentive."

So I sign up for another mountain biking class at Tom's. I don't tell myself it's because I hope to change Hunter's mind about us. I don't want to keep putting off seeing him and I can keep my hopes to myself.

Holding my breath the whole time, I show up at the adventure center. I know Hunter might be my instructor. I haven't seen him since I moved, somehow, even though this town is small.

Instead of Hunter, the first person I see when I arrive is Tom. He smiles at me and nods approvingly at my jersey and padded shorts. I still feel silly, walking around in these shorts like I know what I'm doing. "We'll have you clipping into the pedals eventually," he says.

The idea of being attached to my bike terrifies me, so I shake my head vigorously. That's one thing I'm not planning to try. He laughs.

"How are the tours going? I guess you're switching to winter activities soon."

"That's right—your first winter here! You're in for a treat." Tom shrugs. "We have a lot of new ideas to try this year. Did Hunter tell you? He's my new partner. Obviously the brains behind this whole business. We're launching that subscription model he's been talking about for a year now."

"Really?" My heart skips a beat, knowing this is a big step for Hunter. Even though we don't talk anymore, I can imagine how thrilled he must be. He wanted so badly to prove himself to Tom, and to prove that his ideas were sound for business.

"I'd been thinking about it for a while, truth be told," Tom says. "But he hadn't asked."

I'm sad that I might not get to ask Hunter what inspired him to finally make the ask. I'm so proud of him, even if I have no right to be. Hm, inspire. There's that word again.

"That's great," I say. "I think that's a great decision."

"Well, he made us one repeat customer," he grins, nodding at me as the example. "Few people can do this line of work forever; you need a plan B and hell, maybe he'll end up taking over for me."

"Maybe so," I agree. "Not anytime soon, I'm sure."

"No! This is only the beginning!" He winks. "Anyway, you better get to your class. They're lining up out by the bike shed."

I hustle out to the bike shed, my nerves starting to zing. I haven't been on a bike since I fell off one, and I'm still not sure who my instructor is going to...oh.

Hunter is standing at the shed, helping fit someone to their bike. He turns around and sees me, and I freeze.

He nods at me, a quick chin lift like we're bros at a bar. I swallow and nod back. This is how it's going to be now that we both live in town. We're going to have to see each other casually and not *see* each other. I can do this. This is fine.

He helps me fit a bike, and while we have our heads together, he says quietly. "I wanted to tell you sorry. For treating you like we were just a fling."

"Oh." I pull back. "I didn't think you did that."

"Well, I didn't intend to. But I guess I probably did. And you deserve more than that. So I'm sorry."

Blinking rapidly, I nod. "Thanks," I whisper, and try to come up with something else to fill the awkward void between us, and then someone asks a question and pulls Hunter away.

Once I'm on my bike and we're heading down the trial, I wonder why I signed up for this. It's hard enough keeping my tire on the narrow dirt track; next I'm going to try to climb a rock feature?

Hunter has everyone stop and explains the first feature, then demonstrates riding over it a few times. It's probably a really easy one. It just looks hard to me. Like something a bike tire should never go over. Bikes are for flat surfaces, surely? There's air in these tires. Couldn't they pop?

Everyone else successfully attempts the feature as I stand there watching.

Hunter, who left his bike on the other side, walks over to me. "It's OK to walk it," he says quietly.

"No," I say. "I'm going to try it."

"You don't have to try everything," Hunter replies. "It's OK to say no to things you really don't want to do."

"I do say no when I don't want to. And I say yes when I'm scared."

He nods slowly. "I like that about you."

"Do you?"

"You know I do."

Then he steps back, to let me try.

I panic at the last minute before my tire goes up the rock and brake hard. And then I decide to try again. And then again, when I get stuck half way up because I forgot to downshift.

Hunter waits for me, offering me advice every time I circle back around. "You've got this," he says.

Finally, I stop. "I guess the group is probably getting impatient," I say. "Maybe I can't do this."

"I called Scott to come out and take the rest of the group ahead," Hunter says. "They're fine. You need to session this. You'll get there."

Wondering at his patience, I study his face. Is he like this with everyone? Knowing Hunter, he probably is. I still feel a little special.

Under his watchful gaze, I try again. At least I haven't completely fallen off the bike yet. I catch myself before I go down.

"You're braking before you get to the feature, and it's slowing down your momentum so the bike wobbles and freaks you out," Hunter observes. "Try pedaling through it instead."

It sounds so logical when he says it. *Just pedal through it.* Sounds a lot like life advice.

Maybe I'll never be good at this—or anything—on the first try. I need a lot of advice, a lot of outside observing, in order to get something right.

"Try one more time," Hunter urges me.

So I do. And this time, determined, I don't brake right before I get to the feature. I pedal up and over it, like it's almost effortless, like the bike was waiting for a chance to do it.

I scrape one of my pedals against a rock as I go over it, but Hunter—running after me, up the trail—shouts that it's no big deal. "We'll work on pedal position later!"

After stopping the bike and unbuckling my helmet, I breathe a deep gulp of success. "Wow! I did it! Only a million tries later!"

"The only thing that matters about how many times you tried is you kept doing it," Hunter says, stopping by my side. He's grinning ear to ear. "That was great. Congratulations!"

"You're a great teacher," I reply, smiling widely back at him.

And then I think he almost—not quite—moves to embrace me. And I decide there's another hard thing I might as well try again.

"I've been thinking a lot about sessioning," I say. "Trying something over and over again until you get it right."

He nods, his expression slowly moving from delighted to focused. He's listening.

"And I was thinking, what about us?" I lick my lips, forcing myself to keep going in the face of his neutral expression. "What if we have to session us to get it right?"

"You mean...try again?"

Pressing down hard on my lips to keep my mouth from wobbling, I nod. I'm scared, so I say yes. "I think I've proved I'm willing to keep trying."

"But..." He pauses, and I hold my breath. "Do you really want to? Or do you think trying is the right thing to do?"

Carefully, I put my bike down on the ground, laying it so it's not on the gear shift side, or the "expensive side" as Hunter explained it to me. I stand in front of him, spreading my gloved hands. "I really want to, Hunter. I've learned a little bit lately about listening to my own voice and I think I recognize it now."

I hold my breath, because this might be the last time I try to convince him or it might be the first of many. I'm willing to keep going if I have to.

Then he grins. "I do, too."

"Really?"

"If I have to session us to get it right, I will." He adds with a little smirk, "It might take a *lot* of practice."

Surprised by my own success—I just had to make the ask—I jump into his arms and kiss him. With Hunter, I'm completely willing to practice for the rest of my life.

MOLLIE

ONE YEAR LATER

OF COURSE MY mom's a natural at axe throwing. She picks up everything quickly and must have that "mind-body connection" Hunter is always talking about. Sometimes, when the sex is really good, I think I've achieved it. I'm still struggling with it on any activity with less incentive.

It's my birthday again and a group has gathered at the axe throwing venue. Hunter reserved the entire space for us: Nora and her new boyfriend, Sophie and Chad, Scott, Tyler and Zoe, and my mom. Tom couldn't make it and neither could Mr. Smith and Dorothy, who we invited even knowing they'd be in their pajamas by 8pm.

Hunter hadn't wanted me to invite Nora and Sophie. "They're not real friends," he'd said—his voice gentle because his words weren't. "When have they ever been supportive? They even abandoned you when you needed help moving."

I couldn't imagine my two oldest friends not bearing witness to how much I'd changed my life. I'd invited them while telling Hunter they might not show up. But they both came. And that was something.

After my mom shows off her ability to pick up any activity within minutes, Hunter and Scott wow everyone by throwing two axes at once. I'm pretty sure Nora's new boyfriend is jealous. He definitely isn't going to last for long with that attitude. Nora already looks annoyed.

"Hunter's in an axe throwing league," Nora says dismissively. She's clearly trying to inspire the dude to chill. "Of course he's good."

"Mollie and I throw every week," Hunter agrees good-naturedly. "She's in the league, too."

"*You* are?" Nora and Sophie both turn on me, shocked.

"I am," I say proudly. Hunter had convinced me, building the case that I was good enough over several months of lessons. I'm not the most talented person in our league, but I'm not the worst every week, either. And when Hunter and I throw as a team, we do pretty well.

"Are you going to show us?"

"Show us, show us," Scott, who has been drinking, starts a short chant.

Looking around, I see no sympathy. My mom, who has been in town almost once a month since I moved here—protesting she wants to see her daughter but really exploring the idea of retirement—waits to see me demonstrate skill travels through genetics. Hunter, smiling with quiet confidence in my abilities, waits to see me shut everyone up. Tyler and Zoe, who have heard me bemoan this activity plenty of times, wait to see the hours I've spent on it—and really spent on hanging out with Hunter—pay off.

"I'll show you," I agree. "First, I want to make a toast. To myself."

Everyone laughs. They gamely pick up their plastic cups and hold them up.

"I haven't always been good at listening to my own voice. And this past year has been about learning how to do that. I've been lucky enough to be surrounded by people who let me get quiet and hear myself." I wave my hand at the group around me. Even Nora and Sophie came around to my decision to move. They both think my mom is the least reckless person in the world, so when she decided to buy here, that pretty much won them over.

But Hunter. He's all-in, never once wavering when I need him to back me up on everything from replacing the light switch covers in the condo to trying outdoor climbing—which was terrifying. That's one thing I never need to try again.

Who knows where we'll be in our relationship in another year. I can't ask Hunter to move into my mom's condo and he can't ask me to move into Tom's house. We're enjoying our time together and where we are now, though. Hunter is studying for his MBA and slowly taking over business operations, while Tom focuses on marketing. I am easing into a true friendship with Zoe, who has finally accepted me as a local. We are having a *lot* of sex—up against a wall, hanging over the side of the bed, from behind, from the front. We session what doesn't work and we keep doing what does. We talk about the future sometimes, though without urgency. Like we're following a path that we know leads somewhere nice—somewhere with an epic view— but we're not in a hurry to get there. That's enough.

Tipping my cup at Hunter so he knows I'm thinking of his support in particular, I take a drink. Everyone else says "cheers" and drinks their own.

I pick up my axe. Hunter showed me how to wrap it in tape to fit my own grip. Now it's comfortable for me to hold it, like an extension of my arm. I laughed when Hunter first used that phrase, and yet he was right. A lot of things have become more comfortable for me over the last year. I think I'm generally a more comfortable person with *myself* now.

Trying things is still my "thing," and I don't jump from thing to thing so quickly anymore. I know it's going to take me time to master everything I try, so I embrace the commitment and focus on one thing at a time for a semester or a season or however long it takes.

Sharing a brief grin with Hunter, I decide I'm going to show everybody that I don't just try hard, sometimes—with the right ingredients, and support around me—I succeed.

Yes, says my mind and my body and my heart pounding with excitement that I get to have a birthday party like this, surrounded by people I love in a place I chose. *Yes*.

Lifting the axe over my head with one arm, I aim my elbow at the target and follow it with my eyes. Then, with perfect follow-through, I throw the axe down the center of the lane, flying end over end until it hits the target. Bullseye.

Colorado romance author Alicia Wilder writes about real people finding real love. Welcome to the Telluride Temptations, where imperfect people get happily ever afters. If you enjoyed this book and also want to hear Zoe and Tyler's love story, read about how they met in High On Love: A 4/20 novella. This novella is exclusively available to newsletter subscribers at: https://aliciawilder.com/newsletter/